APACHE CROSSING

APACHE CROSSING

Seven years and a thousand bullets after the train robbery Jed Stevens came back to Apache Crossing. He had waited all this time to claim the $80,000 buried there and he had no intention now of splitting up the loot with his gun-toting confederates. But in this seedy little town Frank Barton was the Law. And Barton had sworn to keep the peace – even if he lost the girl he loved and had to trade lead with his own brother!

APACHE CROSSING

by

Lee E. Wells

The Golden West Large Print Books
Long Preston, North Yorkshire,
BD23 4ND, England.

British Library Cataloguing in Publication Data.

Wells, Lee E.
  Apache Crossing.

  A catalogue record of this book is
  available from the British Library

  ISBN   978-1-84262-962-8 pbk

Published in Large Print 2014 by arrangement with
Golden West Literary Agency

The Golden West Large Print is an imprint of Library Magna
Books Ltd.

Printed and bound in Great Britain by
T.J. (International) Ltd., Cornwall, PL28 8RW

I

The main street of Apache Crossing baked
in the hot Arizona sun. Within the marshal's
office it was comparatively cool, for now
and then a breeze moved through the open
door across Frank Barton's narrow, high
boned face. He listened to the heavy voice
of Sam Yoder, the Pinkerton detective. Now
and then his sharp brown eyes would move
to the beefy, perspiring railroad detective or
the lean banker, who was also president of
the Town Council.

Yoder opened a folded telegram and
passed it to Owen Grange, the banker. 'That
came from Yuma this afternoon.'

Frank's quiet gaze followed the yellow
paper from Yoder to Grange. He sat in the
chair behind the desk, light glinting from
the marshal's badge on his shirt. His
angular face remained calm, only the slight
beat of fingers on one chair arm indicating
troubled thoughts.

He felt deep in his bones this conference
was but the prelude to a long period of

suspense and trouble. Knowing something like this might happen, he had hoped it wouldn't. Now – here it was.

Grange pursed long, dry lips and passed the telegram to Frank. He read the brief message.

'Subject to be released Yuma Territorial to-morrow. Will cover and inform. Garrett.'

Frank passed the wire back to Yoder who had covertly watched him. Frank asked, 'By "subject" they mean Jed Stevens?'

'That's right. Our man, Garrett, has confirmed Stevens' release. He will have served exactly seven years – his full sentence.'

Grange said wryly, 'Rance Bailey didn't.'

'Bailey was paroled three years ago. He broke up a riot and saved the Warden's life. The parole was his reward.'

'What happened to him?'

Yoder shrugged. 'He dropped out of sight. We don't care. Stevens is the man we want – the key. He walks out of prison tomorrow. He'll be covered constantly and when he leaves Yuma in any direction, I'll get a wire.'

Owen Grange said wonderingly, 'You people never give up!'

Yoder grinned, a tight pull of full lips back from large teeth. 'We're paid not to – by the San Francisco banks. Remember, the eighty thousand dollars Stevens stole was their money. It's never showed up. They want it.'

The four men fell silent, each picturing that money, hidden somewhere around Apache Crossing.

Yoder broke the brief silence. 'Mr Grange, Stevens' account in your bank is still intact?'

'Never been touched, even grown a little with seven years' interest.'

'Good. When he leaves prison, he'll have his railroad ticket and five bucks from the Warden. And that'll be about it. So, I'm betting he'll make a draw on that account through a Yuma bank.'

'Should I honor it?'

'Of course! It's his. Just let me know.'

Frank shifted his weight and his holstered gun bumped dully against the rim of the chair seat. He leaned forward elbows on the desk, long, capable hands steepled. 'I didn't know he had an account.'

'Sizable one,' Grange said with banker's reluctance. 'He raked off from every gambler and dancehall girl in town when he was marshal. Might still be doing it, but he got too greedy and pulled the train robbery.'

'That's what I don't savvy,' Frank said slowly. 'If that money was never recovered, why was he allowed to keep the account in your bank?'

Yoder spoke in a condescending way that rankled Frank. 'Marshal, the San Francisco banks could have taken over the account. But it's peanuts compared to eighty thousand dollars.'

His smugness increased. 'What you don't understand is that we want Stevens to find he still has his money. So, he'll be confident we can't touch him, for he pleaded innocent the whole time, remember? He'll move all the faster to get the eighty thousand, wherever he hid it. That's what we want.'

Frank frowned. 'There was always a doubt there.'

'Doubt!' Yoder exploded. 'Hell, we know he was guilty! So did the jury that gave him seven years.'

'No one ever proved it.'

Al Curran mopped the sweat from his round, red face. 'It happened before your time, Marshal.'

'It was all I heard when I first took over Stevens' badge. Lot of argument for and against, I remember.'

Yoder snorted. 'What argument could there be! The train with the San Francisco money shipment was held up and eighty thousand dollars stolen. Two men did the job and one of them was wounded. Stevens was deputy sheriff, besides being Marshal–'

'He beat me there,' Frank smiled faintly.

Yoder's hard eyes flicked at him, no more. 'Stevens and Rance Bailey made up a posse and led it all over hell. Only when the sheriff came and read signs did they find the wounded robber – and he was dying. He talked and implicated Bix Terry–'

'Who tied in Rance Bailey and Jed Stevens,' Grange said distastefully. 'Our marshal and his deputy!'

'It was stated at the trial,' Yoder picked up the story, 'that four of them were in on the deal. Bix and his friend did the actual robbing. They passed the money to Bailey, who brought it to town and passed it to Stevens, who had been all night in the Geronimo Bar – an alibi. He was supposed to have hidden it.'

Curran cut in. 'The idea being, they'd meet when the shouting was over and the posse disbanded. They'd divide the loot and no one would be the wiser. It didn't work that way. Bailey got ten years. Stevens drew seven. Bix Terry had escaped to Mexico. Later, Rance was paroled. Stevens has served his full term.'

Yoder smiled unpleasantly at Frank. 'Who could doubt Stevens was guilty?' He added

11

evenly, 'Unless someone close to Stevens persuaded him.'

Frank slowly lowered his hands to the desk. His angular face grew tight. 'Meaning?'

'You're courting Peg Winters, and she's his step-daughter.'

Frank held himself in the chair by force of will. 'I don't like that. Peg knows no more about this than any of us – maybe less.'

'Frank–' Grange said worriedly.

'I have never let my personal life interfere with my law badge, but maybe you think–'

Grange stood up, distressed. 'I'm sure he didn't, Frank.'

'Do you?' Frank bored at Yoder.

'I'm a detective, Marshal. I have to know how you stand. You'd do the same in my position, especially since one Apache Crossing lawman was sent to Yuma.'

Their eyes locked, Frank's angry. Yoder's smile was bland and friendly, the eyes veiled. Frank asked with deceptive softness. 'And now do you know?'

'I think so, Marshal. I'm satisfied.'

Grange moved hurriedly to the desk. 'Of course he is, Frank. We have every confidence in you. If we didn't trust you, we wouldn't be here.'

'That's right,' Yoder agreed.

'We should all work together,' Grange insisted. 'I represent the citizens and you the law, Frank. Mr Yoder represents the San Francisco banks and Mr Curran the railroad. You and I have an interest in justice, law and order. Yoder and Curran have an interest in the money.'

'And we have to get it,' Yoder said flatly. 'Only Stevens can lead us to it. He's tricky and dangerous. Between us, we'll have to watch him all the time.'

'If he shows up,' Frank suggested.

'Depend on it, he will.' Yoder looked around. 'There's something else you can depend on. We're not the only ones who've counted the days until Stevens' release. There's Rance Bailey. There's Bix Terry. I'll make a bet they'll both show up.'

Owen Grange sighed, 'I think you'd win.'

'They'll flock in,' Yoder said heavily. 'They want eighty thousand dollars – and so do we. We can't make a mistake.'

Frank eased back in his chair. 'I'll work with you – despite Peg Winters.'

Curran, again mopping his face, stood up. 'It's my guess Stevens will come directly here to Apache Crossing. He's smart enough to know he'll be watched by our people for sure, and maybe by some of the gang he tricked. He'll not waste time trying to shake them off.'

'I see it that way.' Yoder slapped his hands on his knees and pulled himself from the chair.

Frank said, 'He has a right to come, you know. He's served his term and is a free citizen again.'

'I know,' Yoder nodded. 'So we leave him alone and watch him.'

'Figuring he'll make a dash for the loot when he thinks it's safe?'

'That's it,' Grange said. 'That's when we'll need a law badge, Frank.'

Frank nodded slightly. The men moved to the open door, braced themselves against the heat and then left. Frank stood by the desk a long moment and then returned to his chair.

His dark brows knotted down as his eyes grew troubled. He looked out on the yellow, hot dust of the street without really seeing it. He suddenly looked much older than his thirty-two years. Little lines formed about the firm mouth and a muscle jumped in a lean cheek.

How much of a strain would Jed Stevens' return put on Frank's romance with Peg? She loved her step-father, even though she more than half believed him guilty. Sometimes she became angry at a chance remark about him. She'd hotly tell Frank so kind a man could not be an outlaw. Again, she'd wonder and doubt. So now Frank couldn't tell how she'd act.

He sighed. He'd have to tell her about this – at least that Stevens was expected. He'd better tell her today, before things started happening.

Frank stirred and glanced at the yellow faced wall clock. Time to make his rounds again. It was Saturday and a lot of punchers had already come in from the surrounding ranches. They'd be drinking and funning now. Despite the heat, he'd best keep a rein on potential trouble. Then he'd see Peg.

He pulled his lean, muscular length from the chair, took his hat from a peg and adjusted the holster to his leg. He squinted his eyes against the sun as he stepped out on the wooden canopied porch, tugging his hat brim to shield his eyes as he moved with long, easy strides down the planked sidewalk.

There were three saloons in Apache Crossing, each serving one of the major social classes. The ranchers and businessmen spent their time at the Cattleman's. Hired hands, punchers and clerks patronized the Geronimo, now and then a chuckline rider or saddle bum. But more often, they went to Manuel Perez' cantina to mingle with the Mexicans.

Frank headed to the cantina. He expected no trouble for the Mexicans were a gentle and happy lot as a whole. Now and then one of them, would let the fiery *aguardiente* get the better of him, but nothing came of it. Manuel saw to that. A swipe of the big fist would fold the erring one under a table or in a corner and Manuel, disarming him, if that were needed, would unceremoniously drop him in the street like an empty sack. If Frank happened by, the sinner landed in jail to repent until morning.

Frank stepped into the thick-walled adobe cantina, saw half a dozen dark men placidly drinking, talking, playing cards. There was a sudden silence at his entrance but a moment later talk broke out again.

Frank walked to the zinc-topped bar where Manuel presided. Manuel was a huge bear of a man, dark of skin, bullet round of head and ugly of face. His dark eyes were gentle and now they lighted in honest warmth.

''*Dias, amigo!*''

16

'Hot day, Manuel.'

'What else in this country, eh?'

Frank leaned against the bar, removed his hat and wiped the sweat from the inner band. Manuel indicated the bottles on the back bar. 'A drink, perhaps?'

'No, thanks. That stuff is hotter than the weather.'

Manuel grinned, displaying a gold tooth. 'Like chili, it makes the heat inside. So, you forgot the heat outside.'

'A hell of a way to cool off!' Frank half turned, practiced gaze lazily circling the room. His eyes caught the crepe-framed picture over the back bar. Within the glass were crumbling flower petals, a small silver crucifix across one corner. The man in the picture had Manuel's features, though there was less of the bull in chest and shoulders. Manuel's eyes followed Frank's and he sighed.

'It is almost seven years ago now, *amigo*, since Ernesto was murdered.'

'Before my time.' Frank added gently. 'You two must have been close.'

'He was my brother – like another part of my soul.'

Frank studied the picture. Here was one of the few unsolved mysteries in the county, undoubtedly a Mexican knifing, a vendetta, a deadly boiling of passion over some woman – anything.

Too bad it had happened during the excitement over the train robbery. Ernesto's killer might have been trailed and caught. Frank straightened. A Mexican, he thought wryly, has as little chance in death as he does in life.

He pushed away from the bar and left with a brief, friendly nod to Manuel. He slowly walked along the street, glad of the shade under the canopies before the stores. More saddle horses were in evidence, more buckboards and buggies. It would be a typical Saturday night. He entered the Geronimo.

The voices were louder here and many of the tables were already filled. The bar had its quota of customers, sun beaten men who drank and played as hard as they worked.

Frank nodded to Jim Gavin, the owner, and his assistant, already busy. He looked about for Flying W hands and a glimpse of his brother. Apparently the outfit had not come in yet. He made sure no one wore a gun, forbidden by a town ordinance. Satisfied, he left.

The Cattleman's was nearly empty. Quiet and more dignified, it was the one place where trouble seldom came. A few ranchers sat at the tables, talking in low voices or con-centrating on the fine art of poker psycho-logy. A glance sufficed and Frank left.

He stood a moment on the shaded porch, looking along the street, eyes moving beyond the bank, the town's single brick structure, and on to the high verandah and sun-reflecting white of the hotel. He studied it a moment, gnawing at his lip, and then, with a mental shrug, stepped out into the sunlight, angling across the street.

The lobby was deserted but he heard the clink of cutlery in the main dining room. A Mexican woman, setting the tables, looked up when he entered and gravely inclined her head toward the closed door that led to the kitchen.

He found Peg busy with mixing bowls and supervising another Mexican woman at the big, black range. Heat filled the room, only faintly relieved by the desert air that stirred through the open, screened windows.

Peg did not see him, her back to the door, floured arms and hands busy. Frank crossed the room, returning the flashing smile of the cook, and kissed Peg on the nape of the neck. She jumped, then returned his kiss, doughy hands held well away from him.

'There's coffee,' she said.

He poured a cup and took it to a table beside an open window. He dropped his hat on the floor, sipped at the coffee while Peg returned to her work. He watched her, struck again with his luck that such a woman loved a puncher turned lawman.

Peg Winters, even in plain work dress and apron, was slender and attractive. He watched the move of her shoulders and his eyes held on the tanned, smooth skin of the nape of her neck, the sweep of soft, blue-black hair piled in natural waves high on a well shaped head.

She used the back of her hand to brush aside a strand of fallen hair as she turned to the woman at the range. Frank followed her flowing walk across the room.

She was a tall girl with a supple and well proportioned body held naturally erect. Her face was a long, soft oval, the skin smooth and unblemished over planed cheeks, the bone structure delicately modeled.

Her mouth missed the formal standard of beauty, a trifle long with little folds in the corners that suggested hidden laughter. The lips were red and soft, the lower slightly protruding, forming a delicate shadow just above the chin. A straight, feminine nose ridged between well spaced eyes, violet, alive and warm.

She gave brief instructions then washed the dough from, her tapering fingers. She came to the table and kissed Frank. She sat down for a few moments' rest. 'I'll have to run you out soon. This is no time for a man to interfere in the kitchen.'

'Sure. I just dropped by.'

'I'm surprised – this time of day.'

He wondered how he could lead into the news. She looked over her shoulder to make sure the baking went right and then turned back to him. 'The town's quiet?'

'Sure – but filling up.'

She had a way of looking directly and deeply at him when she sensed he was troubled and little, subtle lines marred her smooth, high forehead. He made a business of exactly placing the coffee mug on the table. 'Jed Stevens gets out tomorrow.'

After a moment she said, 'Yes, I know.'

'He'll probably come here.'

'Yes – but I've hoped he wouldn't.'

'It's in the cards. He lived here. He used to wear this badge. You're his only family and...'

'And?' She watched him. He worked on the coffee again. 'I know – that stolen money.'

'It must be here. It was never found.'

'So Jed will come for it – *if* he was guilty.'

'That's right – if he was guilty.'

'I've never been sure of that, Frank. What do you think? You've never said.'

He spoke very carefully. 'A jury gave him seven years. He served it to the very last day. If he did commit a crime, he's paid for it. As a lawman. I have no quarrel with him.'

'It's the money, then.'

'Some believe he'll try to get it.'

'Do you?'

'Peg, I don't know. But I'm forced to work with those who do.'

She studied her folded hands. 'I see.'

He extended his hand and touched her arm, a gentle pressure. 'I wanted you to know. I didn't want it to come as a surprise.'

'I knew – all these years he'd be out, even to the day. But, funny somehow, I didn't think it would ever come... So they'll be waiting for him to get the money they *know* he stole. You'll be with them.'

'Helping's a better word. I want nothing of Stevens.'

'But they do. And you and I–' She broke off then added, 'This makes a difference.'

'How?'

'We shouldn't see one another.'

'No!'

'But, Frank–'

He came out of the chair. She looked up and then his anger vanished in a smile and he took both her hands in his. 'Peg ... sweetheart ... listen. Let Jed Stevens come. Let him live here if you wish. But don't let it come between us. You and me – we've broken no law. You're no blood tie of his. Just the chance of your mother's second marriage made him a step-father.'

'But–'

'Don't let it come between us,' he repeated.

'All right, Darling, I'll try not. But–'

'Good!' He kissed her. He returned to his chair and finished his coffee, glanced at the clock. 'Time to get along.'

'Indeed it is! or you and Dane will have no supper.'

'I know better. By the way, I haven't seen Dane.'

'Late start from the ranch, maybe. He'll be around.'

He kissed her and left the kitchen. For a time she stood with fingers to her lips where his firm mouth had pressed. Her eyes grew distant and she saw Jed Stevens as she remembered. She sighed and turned to her work.

When Frank came out on the street, it was even more crowded and the town bustled. Saturday was the high point of the town's business. Frank crossed to the Geronimo and a half a dozen new horses at the rack. They bore the Flying W brand, so his younger brother had arrived at last.

He moved along the street, making the rounds, went to the railroad station when he heard a whistle deep in the passes to the east. The Limited thundered through and Frank returned to the main street and walked back to the Geronimo.

It had filled. Men lined the bar and he couldn't see an empty table. Talk and laughter made a constant, pleasing racket. He glimpsed Dane over in a corner and Frank worked his way through the crowd.

He came to the table. Dane, a small stack of chips, and a whiskey glass before him, studied his cards, made a bet and then looked up to see Frank. The two men bore a striking resemblance.

They both had the same long, supple build, the same brown eyes, except that Dane's held more of a youthful fire and something of rebellion. He was eighteen but already he tried to act the part of a man.

His eyes met Frank's slight frown and

something of anger touched the younger face. Dane nodded, no more, and leaned back in his chair as the betting continued.

Three of the men were working punchers. The fourth was something else – Cass Nolan, powerfully built with a shock of coarse yellow hair that topped a hard granite face. Cold blue eyes regarded his cards and his blunt fingers pushed chips out to meet and top Dane's bet.

Nolan grinned, a peeling back of firm lips against cruel, square teeth. 'Better have it, friend. You're called.'

Dane lost and Nolan swept in the chips. Dane looked up and Frank made a slight motion of his head toward the wings. The kid was out of his depth. Dane's jaw set and he reached for the cards.

Frank checked irritation and waited. Poker and whiskey! Since the kid had this job, he was busting his britches to look like a man. Frank studied Cass Nolan's heavy features and wondered why Dane had so suddenly taken to him.

Nolan had come to Apache Crossing some three months ago and had rented a house at the edge of town. He drank some and gambled a lot, generally winning. That seemed to be his sole occupation. He hinted he had wandered up from around El Paso, might wander on again when he tired of Apache Crossing.

There was nothing against Nolan. He minded his own business, was pleasant in his brusque way and mingled well in the saloons. But some instinct gave Frank the feeling of hidden wildness somewhere.

Dane had taken up with him. Frank had suggested caution once and his brother demanded reasons. Frank could give none.

The game progressed and again Dane lost. Frank caught his brother's attention. Dark, resentful eyes glinted and the boy's lips set in an ugly line. Dane spoke to Nolan in a voice that held a note of belligerence. 'We're playing for peanuts. How about upping the ante?'

'It's your dinero, *amigo*.'

Again Dane's underbrow look cut to Frank, who made another sign toward the door. Dane squared into his seat. 'Up the ante.'

Frank's jaw set in anger. The kid defied him! Slowly Frank exhaled and the tension left his muscles. He turned from the table and walked out.

After supper tonight, he and Dane would have a talk – definite and to the point.

II

The lights from the stores made a bright, pleasing pattern along the dark main street of the town. Riders appeared momentarily, looming large out of the darkness and then fading into it again. Seated alone on the high verandah of the hotel, Frank impatiently watched for Dane to materialize out of the indistinguishable moving shapes. Saturday nights, Dane always had supper with Frank and Peg. He was long overdue and Frank's irritation slowly crystallized into anger.

Light streamed onto the porch from the open lobby door behind him. He could hear faint sounds from the dining room where the twenty or so guests ate. He heard a rustle of cloth as Peg came up. She smiled down at Frank.

'I've fed the wolves. Now it's our turn. Ready?'

'I'd better find Dane. He's late. He should be here.'

'He's probably forgotten. Let him have his fun.'

27

'After you've cooked a good meal for him! He ought to be with us.'

She kissed him. 'Not at all, Frank. He's young. He's probably tired of spending his time with his older brother and me.'

'What's wrong with us?'

'I think we're perfect,' she laughed. 'But Dane would like younger people. Let him find them – maybe a sweetheart of his own. You wouldn't begrudge him that.'

'Well … no. It's just that–'

'Supper will get cold, darling.'

He pulled himself up, capturing her arm and folding it under his. They ate, as usual, in Peg's private rooms. The food was excellent and they were undisturbed. Sounds from the street were muted and pleasant back here, the lamp on the far table gave a cheery glow.

Tonight, the meal was unusually silent. Dane's empty chair and plate bothered Frank. He wondered what to do about Dane. Signs of rebellion had been small but they had increased. There was a slight strain now, as though Dane resented Frank. He thought of the poker game at the Geronimo this afternoon and Dane's unusual absence now – as deliberate as the unspoken challenge in the saloon.

Peg ate just as silently. They finished and she brought coffee from the kitchen, after clearing the table. They sat at ease but withdrawn into troubled thought.

She broke the silence. 'Frank?'

'Yes.'

'About Jed…'

'What about him?'

'I think we should talk about him.'

'We did – this afternoon.'

'Not really – and I've been thinking.' She searched his face. 'He'll be watched the moment he shows up won't he?'

'Well … yes.'

'It'll be your job, most of it.' She waited but he did not reply. Her eyes darkened. 'I've been thinking about that.'

'No point. I'm not going to arrest him.'

'I know, that's not what bothers me.' She traced an aimless design on the table cloth. 'Sam, Yoder, Al Curran, Owen Grange – they want to find that stolen money.'

'Yoder and Curran are paid for it. Owen co-operates because he's a banker and head of the Council.'

'They look to you. What do they think about us – you and me?'

He looked blankly at her. 'What should they think!'

'I'm Jed's daughter and the whole town knows how it's been with us. Do they fully trust you ... because of me? Suppose something goes wrong? They'd blame you. It'd get to the Council and you could be fired.'

'Not a chance!'

'There could be.'

'Peg, how long have I worn this badge?'

'Six years.'

'In that time, Owen Grange and the Council have come to know me pretty well.'

'And me too well. That's why I'm worried.'

His voice flattened. 'Who bought this hotel? Jed Stevens?'

'No, my mother, right after they were married and he brought us here.'

'The town knows that, too. It knows you and Jed are not blood kin. It knows none of the stolen money went into the hotel.'

'But—'

'I'll tell you something. Just a month ago, Owen Grange talked to me about you. He teased me about letting a good girl slip away because I was too stubborn to get married. There's the whole answer, Peg. Marry me.'

Her eyes deepened, softened and her face glowed radiantly. Then the shadows returned. 'That would only make it worse.'

'Why!'

'Jed – the stolen money. Suppose he comes back for it? Suppose he does manage to slip away with it? They'll say you let him.'

'But Grange wouldn't ever–'

'So I won't marry you, darling,' she cut in, 'until we know.'

'You're doing this for my sake but you're wrong. I can keep my life and my badge separate. Grange and the rest know it.'

'Do Yoder and Curran? You met them just three weeks ago. They represent Pinkerton, the big Coast banks and the railroad. If Yoder and Curran will blame you if something goes wrong, I doubt if the Town Council could fight the power behind them.'

He stubbornly shook his head. 'It won't work that way.'

'I pray it doesn't. I pray Jed is as innocent as he claims.'

'So do I. It'll work out.'

'I wish I could be sure.'

There was noise in the hall as the guests left the dining room. The closed door muffled it. Peg would have to help the hired Mexican women to clean up soon. Frank pulled his watch from his pocket, regretfully looked at it.

'I'd better see if the town's holding together. See you later tonight?'

'Of course. I'll be on the porch as soon as the work's done.'

He kissed her and left.

The street was noisier and more crowded when Frank descended the hotel steps. But the noise was carefree with no danger in it. Tired kids wailed from the buckboards along the racks, men laughed at jokes, women spoke in low whispers of dubious doings of their neighbors and clucked in righteous disapproval.

Frank worked his way through the crowd, heading directly for the Geronimo. His irritation with Dane increased, strengthened by Peg's worry about Jed Stevens. Had Dane been at supper, the Stevens talk would have been avoided.

He climbed the steps of the Geronimo porch. Light streamed over the batwings and sound blasted out to the street. He entered the big room and stopped just within the doors.

Every table was taken and the men lined the bar three deep. Others, carrying drinks, moved here and there among the tables and more than a dozen card games went full tilt.

Frank searched the crowd, eyes moving to the far corner where he had last seen his brother. Dane was not there, nor Cass

Nolan. Frank walked slowly to the crowded bar. He moved to the far end and again surveyed the crowded room. Frank frowned slightly, the only sign on his impassive face. He waited until Jim Gavin served some men nearby.

'Seen Dane?' Frank asked. 'I'm looking for him.'

'He left – oh, about two hours or more ago.'

'Alone?'

'I reckon – no, wait. That poker game broke up and he left with Cass Nolan and two-three other fellers.'

'Where?'

Gavin sighed patiently. 'Frank, how would I know?'

'I guess you wouldn't.'

'He wasn't drunk, I saw to that.'

Frank nodded and pushed away. Out on the street, Frank let the crowd jostle him. He wondered where Dane had gone and he didn't like the idea of Cass Nolan. Another point of defiance, like missing supper at the hotel, a regular thing each Saturday.

Frank thought of Manuel's cantina, an unlikely spot. That left the Cattleman's, hardly the place where a hired rider would go, still, Cass Nolan might. Frank headed there.

The Cattleman's was also busy. The

patrons, well aware of their worth and standing, drank and talked quietly of politics, cattle prices and ranch problems. Several poker games progressed with only quiet words about the tables.

Frank's sweeping glance told him Dane was not here. He exchanged a word or two with the bartender, said 'Howdy' to the owner of the big Slash S and started back to the door again.

'Frank!'

Owen Grange, alone at a table, beckoned him over, indicated one of the empty chairs. Frank hid impatience.

'Rest your feet, Frank. Have a drink.'

'I'm on duty.'

'A drink won't hurt. I'll see the Council doesn't fire you.'

Owen chuckled and signalled to a waiter. Frank sensed a command and he sat down, thumbing his hat back from his forehead. The banker wanted to talk, filled with the Stevens business. Frank could only listen and hold a check on his impatience. In a very real sense, Owen was his boss.

Owen went over the conference of the afternoon and he told Frank Sam Yoder might be an irritating man but he was a good detective and had a job to do.

'He doesn't know you, Frank. This business will soon be over and he'll be gone. Work with him.'

'Sure, Owen.'

'Pinkerton's a big outfit and there might come a time when both you and me will need them. Like the San Francisco banks need them now.'

Frank grunted, shot a sidelong glance toward the distant door. Owen leaned back, face bemused and spoke with awe in his voice. 'Eighty thousand dollars! Never found! I keep thinking, suppose it had been consigned to my bank.'

'You were lucky.'

'Indeed I was! I wonder where Stevens could've hidden it.'

'Maybe he didn't.'

The banker waved that aside. 'You can bet he did. The whole thing hangs together too well. He hid it, all right. I guess I'm like the rest – wondering where. I've been wondering for seven years.'

'Maybe we'll find out soon.'

'I helped the sheriff hunt for it in every likely place. In seven years, there must've been a couple of hundred people who've dug, burrowed and everything else – nothing.'

'Owen–'

'Practically tore his place apart. You've been out there, haven't you?'

'Yes, but–'

'It was nice once, out there just beyond the town limits. But in seven years, the yard's been dug up and turned over half a dozen times. They've punched holes in the walls and torn up most of the floors. The outbuildings are a wreck. And not one dollar has ever been found.'

Frank's patience slipped. He stood up abruptly. 'No point in us chewing on it tonight. We'll take care of Stevens and the money in due times.'

'Of course, but–'

'It's Saturday night. I better see that things keep quiet.'

Owens' dry face tightened but he only nodded. Frank sensed the man's displeasure, but it was done. He thanked Owen for the drinks and left.

It took but a few minutes to reach the *cantina* and even fewer to see that Dane was not there, either. He left the adobe building, the tinkling notes of a guitar following him, its gay notes a contrast to his angry mood.

He stopped at the next corner, puzzled. He had covered every likely spot Dane could be. He wondered if the boy had gone to Cass Nolan's place, a rented cottage on the other side of town.

Frank made an angry grimace. The boy defied him. It was time to pull him up short. Maw had given Frank control of him when she died. She had warned that Dane's paternal bad blood might show up, worried about it to her last breath.

Frank scowled along the crowded main street. He thought of Peg. By now her work would be over and she'd be on the dark porch, waiting. Frank started toward the hotel.

A block further, a side street led off to the railroad station, crossed the tracks and continued as a road into the open range. As Frank crossed it, he saw Cass Nolan coming up the side street. Frank stopped on the corner, waiting.

The big man reached the corner and Frank moved to intercept him. Nolan stiffened and then identified Frank by the light streaming out of the drygoods store. 'Evening, Marshal.'

'Have you seen Dane?'

'Why, yes, I have.'

Nothing more. Frank kept his voice level. 'Mind telling me where?'

37

'Course not.' Nolan jerked a thick thumb over his shoulder, back the way he had come. 'He's at Millie's.'

'Millie's!'

Beyond the railroad tracks stood a rambling frame building, secretive by day and blinds drawn at night. Here Millie and her four girls entertained the male citizens of Apache Crossing.

Frank couldn't quite keep the tremble out of his voice. 'Did you take the kid there?'

Nolan's heavy face grew tight. 'He walked on his own two legs, Marshal. Anything else you want to know, ask Dane. Me, I don't have to account to you for what the kid does.'

Frank's fists clenched. The man was right and Frank could do nothing, much as he wanted to. He took a deep breath and stepped around Nolan.

'Marshal, just one more thing.'

Frank wheeled about. 'What?'

'I'll make it clear. A bunch of us decided to go to Millie's. Dane came with us and no one persuaded him or forced him. There's nothing wrong in a man doing what he pleases. Something you ain't learned, Marshal. To some people, Dane's a man.'

Nolan turned on his heel and strode away,

every move showing contempt and inward, derisive laughter. Frank stood a long moment, every muscle tense, anger flaming.

Then, with a muffled oath, he whipped around and strode down the dark side street toward Millie's discreet adobe.

III

Heat was a substance that filled the hard packed area from the administration building to the big main gate, where a prison guard watched Jed Stevens approach. The guard's smile was as false as the cool promise of black shadows among the grim buildings.

Beneath the new black, wool suit, Jed sweated and itched, and the white shirt clung like a soggy plaster to his slender, muscular back and chest. He carried a carpetbag, light with his few belongings.

The guard swung open the last barrier and Jed looked through the gate upon the shimmering infinity of the desert. Already freedom felt strange after seven years of surveillance. It took deliberate thought to walk steadily to the guard, to grin in answer to the smile pasted on his lips.

'Well, Stevens, it won't be the same without you.'

'You'll get along.'

'Sure. We ain't losing *all* our happy family.

How long do you figure to be gone?'

'Do you think I plan to come back?'

'Most of 'em do. Why are you any different?'

Jed smiled, a twist of long lips under the narrow, iron gray mustache. 'Now that's a question ain't it? But I think I've got the answer.'

'Until your free-money runs out. Enjoy it while you can.'

He waved, jestingly ceremonious, and Jed walked into the shadow of the arch, out into the blinding sunlight again. The great gate closed behind him, the sound of it reminding him of the time he had entered here so long ago.

He stood on the brow of a high hill overlooking a river that cut a green swath through a desolate land. The road dropped steeply to the desert floor and, a mile or so to his left, the adobe and frame buildings of the town crouched against the impact of the heat.

He felt a cynical twinge of disappointment. How many times he had thought Rance Bailey and Bix Terry would be waiting right here with meaningless words of welcome and friendship? How many times had he imagined how he would play them for what they were worth and then cut away and head straight as an arrow for the cache?

All for nothing, since they weren't here – or anyone else. But they would be – somewhere. Rance and Bix wouldn't let him be lonely nor would others, many others, unknown as yet. The scent of money. Like that of carrion, gathered the buzzards.

Jed tugged his hatbrim lower over flecked, golden eyes and looked back at the prison. Its high, grim walls stood in silent mockery and Jed's thoughts mocked in return. Heat, cold, cruelty, riot and death had not overcome him. Here he was, outside – and outside he was going to stay.

He walked down the slope of the hill, his heavy shoes kicking up puffs of coarse sand. He looked down on the river, at the railroad trestle that bisected it, at the lumbering ferry working its way to the far shore and another state.

Jed swiped tapering fingers along a lean cheek, then cuffed his hat back on his high forehead. Maybe it would be smart to cross the desert and get lost in the towns along the Coast. He considered, biting at his lip, and then rejected it. It would only defeat the showdown. Rance and Bix had only to wait, something they had done for seven years. Best to go on as he had so carefully planned and take no chance in losing what prison, time and patience had earned for him.

He hefted the carpetbag and moved on down the hill. He was not a tall man and looked even smaller in the immensity of yellow desert and brazen sky. The black, coarse suit made him look slimmer and he walked with a suppleness that belied his forty-five years.

He turned toward the town, still half expecting to find watchers. There were none and he stopped, dropping the carpetbag and taking a deep breath, filling his lungs, for the first time enjoying freedom. It wouldn't last, he knew. In minutes, hours, a day at the most, he'd be watched more closely than ever in prison.

He picked up the bag and strode on, disregarding the heat. He came to the first adobes of the town and then the stores. He entered the plaza and stopped on a corner, searching along the wooden canopied buildings surrounding the square. His eyes lighted on a sign and he moistened his lips as he moved on.

The interior of the saloon was a dark,

blessed relief from the blazing morning sunlight. Jed caught the sharp smell of beer as he pushed through the batwings and his nostrils dilated to the delight of it. He strode to the bar, where a single customer and an attendant eyed him.

He smiled and spoke a cheerful 'Howdy' that they answered with reserved nods. The bartender waited, arms spread and braced. Jed looked carefully at each bottle on the backbar shelves.

'It's all whiskey, friend,' the bartender said at last.

'So it is, and a lot of it. What's the best?'

The man placed a bottle and shotglass before him. Jed placed a new five dollar bill on the bar. The bartender watched as Jed sipped the drink, savoring its hot flavor. Then he downed the rest in a single gulp and the shock made him gasp and his eyes water.

The bartender said, 'Best go at it slow – after all that time away from it.'

Jed stared, bottle poised. 'How do you know?'

'The new bill – and take a good look in the mirror. Now and then you gents come in, fresh from up on the Hill.'

Jed looked in the mirror. His skin was

pale. There was a hard set to the jaw and a glint in the eyes, but prison had put no other stamp upon him. Age had, though, in the flecks of gray in mustache and dark hair at the temples. His forehead was a little higher, too.

Maybe in other ways? It had been a long time since he had topped a bronc or had a gun in his hand. A little less speed and stamina? He grimaced, downed the drink, felt the heady bite of it much more quickly than he used to.

Jed pushed from the bar. 'Where's the telegraph office?'

He followed directions, strolling under the continuous wooden canopies before the stores, looking in windows, knowing he could walk or loiter as he willed. He found the telegraph office and turned in.

A long nosed clerk with a green eyeshade and black sleeveguards met him at the counter, checked Jed as he reached for a blank and a stub pencil. 'Paid or collect, Mister? Some of you – some come in and send wires hoping they'll be paid for on the other end.'

'Some of us fresh down from the Hill?' Jed slapped money on the counter and rapidly wrote on the blank.

45

'Territorial Bank of Apache Crossing,' the clerk read, 'Send two hundred dollars local bank by return wire. Charge to my account. Johnson – Jed – Stevens.'

As the clerk turned to send the wire, Jed halted him. 'Next time, friend, be polite and say "Yes, sir". Understand?'

The clerk looked into the golden eyes. 'Yes, sir.'

On the planked sidewalk under the canopy again, Jed listened to the busy click of the telegraph key. He grinned, thinking he would be the first to spread the news of his own release. He could see the flurry at the Geronimo and the Cattleman's – if they were still there. He sobered at the thought of the changes that must have taken place. How did Peg look now? He dismissed that with the thought that one thing hadn't changed. And only he could find that.

Cheered, he moved on, angling across the square and entering the saloon again. He looked back over the batwings. A boy came out of the telegraph office and hurried away, intent on a specific destination. Jed smiled. So! They watched him, keeping out of sight, those bank and railroad detectives.

He went to the bar and ordered another drink. He lifted the glass to the bartender.

'To law and order – firm, steady and predictable!'

'Now that's a hell of a toast from someone–' The bartender caught himself.

'Aint it!' Jed agreed affably, paid and left.

He found a hotel and was pleased that from his upstairs room he could look across the dusty street to the sunbaked front of the bank, green blinds drawn against the glare.

Shedding all but long underwear, Jed stretched out on the bed. The heat wrapped around him. Size of room, hardness of narrow bed and infernal weather – he could close his eyes and it would be as if he had never left the prison. He did and, sure enough...

He awakened suddenly and stared at the bilious wall paper. Then he remembered and swung his legs to the floor, yawning widely. From the slant of the sun and the baking quiet of the street, he knew it must be far into the afternoon. He splashed tepid water on his face from the china pitcher and bowl on a stand.

He dressed leisurely, not bothering with his coat. He crossed the street, empty of all life but himself, and entered the bank. He went to the open door of the president's office. A portly man with a red, sweating face irritably looked up from a big desk.

'Have you heard from the bank at Apache Crossing?' Jed asked.

'Should I?' the man snapped.

'Why, yes, by now – concerning two hundred dollars.'

'Who for?'

'Johnson Stevens, known as Jed.' Jed inclined his head in the direction of the prison. Just come down from the Hill, as you folks say around here.'

The man came to the door. 'How do I know you're Stevens?'

'The same way the bank back there did when it wired you to pay me. Johnson instead of Jed. There's not five people in the Territory know my real first name.'

'All right.' The president edged around Jed and went behind the counter. Jed strolled to the wicket as the teller listened to his boss and threw a covert, alarmed look at Jed. He counted out the money, frowning as grimly as the president. But Jed saw the slight nervous flutter of the teller's hands and the way the president eyed him, staying near a desk with an open drawer that obviously held a concealed gun.

Jed deliberately recounted the money and then stuffed it in his pocket as the two men

48

threw nervous, hopeful glances at the door. Jed placed his hands on the counter.

'You've heard of me?' Both men nodded and Jed smiled. 'Fame! It sure gets around.'

'Are you finished, Mr Stevens?' The president's chubby fingers touched the edge of the desk above the drawer.

'Edgy, ain't you? And all for nothing. I don't rob banks.'

He gave them a mocking salute and strode out into the blasting heat. The money felt good in his pocket, along with the railroad ticket. He went to the saloon for another drink before he found a store where he bought a gray suit of soft material. He bundled up the prison clothing and shoved it in the clerk's hands.

'Send it back to the Hill or give it away. There's no stripes on it but it sure has the prison smell.'

That night, after the first tasty meal he had eaten in years, Jed went to the saloon and then, when darkness fell, to the edge of town and looked at the distant, high prison lights. They went out early and Jed laughed aloud. He made a derisive gesture with wagging fingers and then turned to the warm, welcome lights of the town.

Late that night he crossed the plaza square

toward his hotel. He felt the warmth of whiskey, a sense of complete release. He softly whistled the tune one of the girls had played for him on a piano in a discreet house on the edge of town.

He spoke aloud in self-approval. 'Forty-five years old and you still surprised 'em!'

The hotel clerk stirred from sleep in a big lobby chair when Jed entered, gave him a grumpy look and settled to dreams again. Jed went up the stairs and along the hall to his room. He fitted the key in the lock, opened the door and then stopped dead still.

Only a faint light came from the window but Jed's instinct warned that something was wrong. He could feel it, as he had in the old days. After a moment, that sixth sense told him there was no one in the room and he eased inside and softly closed the door. He cautiously stepped to the ancient dresser and the lamp upon it. He struck a match, lit the lamp and looked about.

The carpetbag was in a different place and open instead of closed as he had left it. The door to the narrow, empty closet was open and the bed disturbed. Whoever had searched had not been careful.

Jed dropped his hat on the dresser and

slowly shrugged out of his coat as he looked around. He sucked in his cheeks and his flecked eyes danced and glittered. Finally he laughed, a soft but grim sound.

The fools! They surely hadn't expected to find anything! Yet they had searched, giving him certain proof that he would be watched and trailed. The doubly dense fools! Did they think he would leave any sign or clue? He had his memory, didn't he? What they sought was in his brain and nowhere else – the knowledge of where eighty thousand stolen dollars were hidden.

If he was killed, the knowledge would go with him. This was his guarantee of life. They didn't dare kill him, any of them, from Rance Bailey to the man or men who had searched this room.

He straightened the bed, sat on the edge and untied his shoes. He paused, frowning at the threadbare carpet, one shoe in his hand. Maybe he'd better buy a gun. It would be an extra margin of safety.

His hand instinctively touched his waist. It had been a long time since he'd worn belt and holster and he'd nearly forgotten the weight of a gun strapped to his leg. Had he also lost his gun speed?

He undressed and rolled into bed, after

51

blowing out the lamp. Get a gun, he decided. Between here and Apache Crossing and in the waiting days to follow, he'd regain his old speed and accuracy.

IV

Only Marshal Frank Barton moved along the street on that bright Sunday morning. The brilliant sun made the adobe and frame buildings frayed and dirty, tight closed now and withdrawn. The saloons were closed and the doors of Zion Church would not be unlocked for two hours. Both good and evil were in abeyance while the citizens of Apache Crossing slept.

Frank hadn't slept well and he needed rest. He was discouraged and he should have been angry. But that was gone now, the dark angel he had finally subdued in the dark morning hours.

He approached his combination of office and jail, his eyes gritty and his brain petulantly demanding sleep. He had the usual quota of week-end prisoners, lodgers rather, for none of them were charged with felony or misdemeanor. A drunk was safer sleeping it off in a cell than in a street or an alley.

Frank paused before he fitted the key in the lock and looked down the peaceful, empty street. He had always made it a practice to release his sorry bunch in time to nurse their hangovers and clean up, hoping their contrition would be strong enough that the church bell would have special meaning. It seldom did, but Frank gave it the opportunity.

He had a few stern words for each sad-eyed man, but this morning one of them required special handling. Frank sighed, turned the key in the lock and entered. He crossed the office to the cell block. There were eight cells, built when Apache Crossing had more than its share of bad men. They were something of a luxury now.

Frank went to the first. He heard a stir along the block, a cursing moan further down. He threw open the door and jerked his thumb toward the outer door as a gaunt-eyed Mexican looked sickly up at him.

'Pedro, the next time you'll stay a week, so help me!'

The man swayed as he stood up and then, gathering strength, scuttled out. Frank continued down the line, giving stern warning to each but hardly knowing what he said, too much aware of the one in the last cell.

Finally, five were gone and Frank slowly approached the remaining locked door. He looked through the bars at the long, slender figure on the bunk. He opened the door.

'All right, Dane. Go into the office.'

The boy glared. Frank waited. At last Dane swung his legs to the floor, saw his hat below the bunk and carefully placed it on his head. He gave his brother a searching, underbrow look and walked into the corridor.

Frank felt pity for him. He remembered how it had been long ago when he had tangled with the rotgut and had awakened the next morning to a cruel and sickening world.

He could understand, and yet Dane must not feel that understanding meant excusing. Frank had to bring this to a halt here and now or all the years of love, hope and training would be lost. He might condone an occasional binge, except that it might be the first sign that Uncle Jim Barton's bad blood worked in Dane. Maw had warned Frank about that before she died.

'He looks like your Paw's brother,' she had said. 'Please, Frank! See that he doesn't turn out the same way!'

Now Frank slowly followed after Dane, who had disappeared into the office. He wondered how he could reprimand and advise without arousing defiance. Dane was already resentful, probably felt like hell, and the wrong word would set things off.

Frank came into the office. Dane sat on a corner of the desk, his head hanging. He lifted it and Frank saw red, pain filled eyes.

'I bet you feel like a big, important man this morning!' Dane burst out. 'Arresting your brother like any drunk Mex in an alley!'

'I'll forget that, Dane.'

'I bet you will! It'll be the first time.' The boy glared, hollow eyed.

Frank walked to the window and looked out, clasping his hands tightly behind his back. He spoke when he knew all anger was out of his voice. 'What did you expect me to do?'

'We got a home – right down the street. What's wrong with that?'

'Nothing. But you were drunk, loud and trying to pick a fight with Tex Baker when I found you.' His voice quivered with the shame of it. 'Did you know that Millie was about ready to send for me? What a hell of a place to make a damned fool of yourself!'

Frank turned. Dane still sat on the corner of the desk, his head down, staring at the floor, biting at his lips. Frank sighed.

'Dane, people look to me to keep the town clean. I'm paid to do a job. I put five drunks in here to keep them quiet and sleep it off. You were the sixth – and the noisiest, trouble-hunting one of the lot. Do you realize that?'

Frank continued, 'Suppose I'd have let you go, shut my eyes to it? What would the town think of its marshal? Are you any different than the others?'

Dane eased off the corner of the desk. He looked sullen but Frank sensed he was at last shamed, Frank placed his hand gently on Dane's shoulder.

'Let's say it's over and done with. You understand what I had to do. I didn't like it, for I expected better things of you.'

He felt the sudden stiffening of the shoulder. He had touched anger but he knew that he had to get some glimmer of his pride, worry and love across. Fear drove him, and disappointment.

'I've tried to teach you to lift your head and walk tall. You know a drunk is a man without pride and without guts. So I was hurt when I saw you that way. On top of that – at Millie's! Dane, you've been brought up better!'

Dane flung away from under his hand, his

young face dark red in angry shame. He started to the door but Frank's sharp command halted him in mid-stride.

'Where are you going?'

'Out – just out!'

'We're not through talking.'

Dane swallowed hard, his eyes flashed. Then he smiled, an unpleasant twist of the lips. 'Why can't we just let it be?'

'Because I don't want this to happen again. And it won't. I'll see to it.'

'How'll you do that, Frank? Talk – because I've grown too big to larrup with a razor strop anymore?'

'You're still my kid brother and–'

'You won't let me forget it. I'm grown. I do a man's work for a man's pay. If I made a damn fool of myself last night, it's because you won't let me learn how to be a man.'

'Dane, you're talking to me!'

'Sure! And I'm still in knee pants and barefoot! I ain't supposed to take a drink, play cards or look at a girl. I ain't growed yet!'

The boy's angry words caught Frank in a trap between error and truth. He couldn't deny and he couldn't admit. He looked upon stark, open defiance, something he had not been prepared to meet. A shred of reason warned that anger and churning emotions offered no chance to reach the boy and yet he never wanted to look weak in Dane's eyes.

'Maybe we'd better let this go for now,' he said coldly. 'Go home and clean up. Get something to eat and try to pull yourself together. We'll discuss this later.'

Dane shifted his weight, nodded and again started to the door. Once more Frank stopped him. 'You missed supper last night, among other things. Peg expects you for dinner late this afternoon. So do I. Maybe by then—'

'I don't want to, Frank.'

'Why not? Don't you like Peg?'

'Yes ... she's all right. I got nothing against her.'

'What then?' Frank added with a touch of contempt, 'Maybe you like Cass Nolan's company better?'

'Maybe I do! One thing I can sure say for Cass. He knows the difference between a man and a boy.'

Dane flung out and the door slammed behind him. Frank jerked it open, saw Dane striding away. Frank's lips parted angrily to order him back and then snapped shut. He stepped back and slowly closed the door.

He dropped heavily into the chair behind his desk. What had happened? What was this new, ugly strain between him and the boy? Frank had tried so hard to shape him into the kind of man of whom Maw would have been proud.

Where had he gone wrong? He had watched Dane closely all through the years. He had encouraged the growth of the strong traits, had tried to teach by word and example those things that led to character and worth. He had seen to it, for instance, that the boy's schooling was the best to be had in these frontier towns.

He had taught Dane how to handle a gun, how to ride, instilled in him the lessons of honesty and the other virtues. Frank had watched closely for Uncle Jim's weaknesses, dealing sternly with the first faint signs, trying to stamp them out.

But perhaps the old saying was true. A boy needed a mother. An older brother was like a trail brand, all right but not the real thing. Should he have married when Dane was small?

The Sunday morning quiet pressed in, forcing Frank to think. Was there still time for a woman to shape Dane and make a home? Maybe even now that would change the boy, settle him, take him from this new course.

Frank pictured Peg Winters. She would certainly be good for Dane – if he would allow her. Dane had shown a coldness toward Peg, a politeness that might conceal dislike. Frank couldn't understand it. A couple of times Frank had seen hurt in Peg's eyes when the boy rebuffed her. She was a good woman, the first in all these years whom Frank had really loved.

Maybe if Dane was forced to be with her, he'd see what a fine person she really was. Maybe if he had a talk with Peg and she really put herself out to be nice to Dane, he'd come to know her as Frank did.

He heard a step on the wooden porch and the door swung open. For a hopeful moment Frank thought it would be Dane, returning to make his peace. But Sam Yoder stepped in.

He removed his bowler and dabbed at his forehead with a handkerchief. 'Going to be another hot day.'

'That time of year,' Frank said shortly.

Without invitation, Yoder dropped into a chair before the desk. 'Might be a hot town before long.'

'What do you mean?'

'The buzzards are coming. Guess who rode in early this morning? Jed Stevens' old friend and deputy – Rance Bailey.'

'Bailey!'

'Tied down guns and all.'

V

Frank jerked upright. 'Where is he now?'

'Rode out to Jed's old place. But I have a feeling he'll be back before the day's over.'

Yoder weighed and judged Frank's reaction, the sallow face bland but probing.

'I suppose you want me to do something,' Frank said.

'Why, no … just keep an eye on him. I thought you'd like to know he's in town.'

'Thanks,' Frank said drily.

Yoder slowly turned his bowler hat in his hand. 'The first one's come and I give it less'n a week before Stevens is here, and others we don't know about yet. Every one of 'em looking for eighty thousand dollars.'

'So are we.'

'Yes – Al Curran, you and me.' Yoder stood up. 'And we have to get it. There's no other way.'

'A tall order.'

'Between the three of us, I don't see how we can miss. We'd better not, if we like our jobs.' He looked about the office. 'Sometimes I wish I was not running all over the country.'

Yoder's eyes grew sharp. 'Your second term, isn't it? Running for election again?'

'No, the Town Council hires me by contract.'

'It'll be renewed?'

'It was once.'

'Mmm ... yes. Depends on what happens, doesn't it?'

Yoder went to the door, looked back and walked out. The man had a way of making things plain without saying the words. He threatened and yet couldn't be accused of it. Frank made a distasteful grimace at Yoder's unspoken arrogance. Surely, Yoder's job hadn't made him that way. He must have had a basic talent for it.

The sound of the church bell aroused Frank. While he sat here with his troubles, the town had come to life for a new day and he had a job to do. Frank walked out on the porch and stood in the shade of the canopy. He first looked toward the Geronimo. There were no horses at the rack, nor at the one before the Cattleman's.

Frank started his routine patrol. At each store building, he tested the door, seeing that it was locked. At the far end of the business district, he cut around to the alley and returned that way. Half of his patrol finished, Frank stood across from Manuel's *cantina*. Cheap paint scabbing from the adobe, the two small windows caked with dirt, the place looked like an ancient crone with a hangover. Frank crossed the street and entered.

Manuel sat in sleepy solitude behind the bar. The odor of stale tobacco, sour wine and the residue of sweat struck Frank like a blow. The floor was thick with dirt, gritty under his boots. Manuel roused at his entrance.

''*Dias, Senor.*'

'Morning, Manuel. You had no trouble last night?'

'I have very good customers – mostly.'

'But you're going to have trouble now.'

Manuel's sleepy eyes flew open. '*Senor?*'

Frank gestured about the room. 'It's filthy. Clean it up.'

Manuel looked pained. 'It is *por nada, Senor.* There will only be more dirt tonight.'

'And it'll soon push you out in the street. Clean it up or close up. It's a menace to health. You have a broom?'

'*Si,*' Manuel said in weary surrender. He pulled himself from the stool, went to the hallway beyond the bar. Frank looked around, nose wrinkling. Manuel returned with a broom so stubby that it was nearly useless.

'That's not worth a damn, Manuel. Buy another.'

Pain added to pain in Manuel's expression. 'That is not good, *Senor*. I must sell many drinks to pay for it.'

'Then do it. Now, start cleaning up.'

Manuel shrugged and moved the stiff broom along the base of the bar. Frank sat on a stool, having trouble concealing a grin. Manuel sighed and struggled, moved under Ernesto's picture.

Frank sobered. Unsolved crimes bothered him. 'No clue as to who killed Ernesto, was there?'

Manuel seizing the excuse, stopped sweeping. 'Marshal Stevens had time only to look around when word came of the robbery. After that…'

'He had troubles of his own.'

'*Si*, a weakness for money. But that is true of all of us, *amigo*. Other than that, he was a very good *jefe*. He would have found who killed Ernesto. That I know.'

'I guess so. Too bad.' Frank stood up. 'Manuel, the floor. You've just started. I'll be back later to see how it looks.'

'It will be crowded then – and perhaps dirty again.'

'Then just keep sweeping. I'll be back.'

Outside and well away from the building, Frank chuckled and shook his head. He sauntered the scant block to the sign that marked the town limits. Below it was a smaller sign.

'No firearms may be carried within the town limits,' Frank read the familiar words. 'Place your Colt in saddlebag and keep rifle in scabbard, or check them with the Marshal. Violation will mean fine, jail or both.'

Frank finished his patrol. He met town families on the way to church. Buggies sedately rolled along, their occupants dressed for worship. A puncher rode by on his way out of town, his week-end over.

Frank returned to his office, loitered a few moments and then started home. Wills, owner of the Running W, came out of the Cattleman's and the rancher motioned him over.

'Morning, Frank. Too early for a drink?'

'Too early – and I'm on duty.'

'Maybe next time, then. Thought I'd tell you Dane's working out.'

'I'm glad he's making it.'

'Good boy there, Frank.' Wills frowned. 'Who's Cass Nolan?'

'Stranger. Don't know much about him. Why?'

'Him and Dane pair up, I notice. Well, got to get on.'

He nodded and walked to the livery stable. Frank moved slowly on. He was pleased to hear that Dane measured up at the Running W but here was Cass Nolan's sign again. Might do to look into him, but no point in telling the boy.

Frank's cottage was a pleasant little structure beyond a row of three paloverde trees. He turned in the walk, glanced toward the barn and saw Dane's horse tethered just before the small stable. Inside, Dane carefully combed his hair at a mirror in the kitchen. Frank cast a quick look his way and turned to the stove, lifting and shaking the granite coffee pot.

'Had coffee yet?' he asked.

'Don't want any.'

Frank filled the pot while Dane finished combing his hair and adjusted a bright kerchief about his neck. Frank tried to show there was no hard feeling. 'Going to be hot today.'

A grunt in reply, no more.

'Dressing up like you're going out sparking.'

'Nope.'

'I'd think some girl would be setting her cap for you.'

'Not likely.'

Frank flipped his finger against the pot to test its warmth. 'When you riding out?'

'Sometime tonight, I reckon.'

'By the way, I hear you're doing pretty good out there.'

'I guess.'

Frank felt a prickle of anger but suppressed it. 'Wills just spoke about you. Asked about Cass Nolan. What do you know about him?'

Dane stood quite still and Frank saw, reflected in the mirror, the tightening of his face. 'Are we going to argue about him again?'

'I'm tired of arguing, Dane. Wills asked about Nolan and I couldn't tell him anything. So, I'm asking you.'

Dane spoke carelessly. 'I guess he's a puncher, wandering through.'

'He's been here for three months,' Frank suggested dubiously.

'Maybe he saved his pay or had good luck with the cards, I don't know.'

'Might pay you to find out. Where's he from?'

'New Mexico – Texas somewhere that-away.'

'Planning what?'

Dane turned sharply. 'I don't know. I don't ask. He treats me like a friend and that's enough.'

'For now, maybe. But–' Frank cut himself short. 'What'll you be doing today?'

Dane took his hat from the table. 'I don't know. Be around, that's all.'

He left before Frank could say anything more. Frank fretfully swiped his hand across his mouth and went to the cupboard for a mug. He filled it with steaming coffee and sat down at the table, leaning back in the chair and staring out the window at the distant yellow rocks of the Chiricuhuas, hardly aware that he looked.

Touchy as a rattler, that boy! Had the quick anger of Uncle Jim. Hope to God he didn't have any of the rest. Frank sipped his coffee and again looked out the window, seeing the past instead of the distant mountains.

Where had he made the wrong turn with Dane? Maybe if he had stayed on as foreman of the Diamond Bar and not accepted the law badge... He shook his head. Maybe –

but that wasn't the whole answer. He cast further back.

How could you peg down anything? Something happens because something happened, and it goes back and back. Even before birth, like the wild Barton streak in Uncle Jim. Never showed up in Paw though, even to the day he died.

Maybe that was when it started. Frank had been seventeen and Dane just three. That was – fifteen years ago! Frank had gone to work, raw kid on a small spread. His pay helped Maw get along, what with her dressmaking and the little money Paw had left.

Hard years, hard work. There was Frank, a boy trying to hold down a man's work and – come to think of it – doing a fair job. He thought of Maw moving to the small cowtown with Dane and looking forward to Frank's coming in from the range on Saturdays.

After a couple of years, she and Frank decided a bigger town would give Maw more work and maybe Frank could do better. They had moved. It was easy for Frank to hire on with a big outfit. That country up around Gallup had been plagued by rustlers and Frank recalled the time he had helped the boss wipe out the gang. Maybe it had started then.

Frank had a natural speed and accuracy with a gun. The boss boasted about him, and word got around. Two years later, Frank was offered the job of deputy sheriff. Maw had been afraid, he remembered, but the job paid good, a lot more than bunkhouse and beans.

He held the job down in a tough country. It gave him the right, if he wanted, to notch his gun three times. He hadn't. Then Maw had suddenly died.

Frank grew somber as he recalled the talk they'd had not a week before her funeral. It was one of those rare moments when she was free of pain and she knew what was to happen. No fear, either, just worry about Dane.

'You're fine, Frank. But Dane worries me and I wonder what will become of him.'

'He's skittish now, Maw, and full of the devil. But he's only ten – just a colt. It'll pass.'

'See that it does, Frank. Promise me?'

'Sure, Maw, but–'

'Even now, he looks and acts like Jim Barton. Funny about blood – you never know where the bad will show up. Like

Andrew and his brother. Andrew was honest, hard working, a good husband. Jim's in trouble or jail half the time. Never settles down. Itchy heel and a mean temper. Fights. He'll get killed someday. I don't want Dane to be like that.'

'He won't be.'

'You've promised, Frank. You've promised your mother.'

'I've promised.'

Within the week she died and within two years Jim Barton won a forty-four slug in his throat instead of chips in a poker game. Maw's dying, prophetic vision had come true and made Frank watch his younger brother all the more closely.

He had tried to provide a home, to send Dane to school and train him in those things schools could never teach. There had been Indian and Mexican housekeepers. There had been wandering from law job to law job, each a little better. And now, Apache Crossing. There had been girls he might have married, but didn't. There had been nothing like love – until Peg Winters. He even hesitated here because of Dane – and that was not fair to Peg.

Frank stirred, brought back to the present. He glanced at the empty coffee mug and then up at the small clock that ticked busily on the opposite wall. Time to make his rounds again and then go to the office. He hitched at his gunbelt and left the house.

He first went to the office, then strolled by the hotel. There was a sudden racket as two dogs vented their dislike of one another and then one of the animals fled with a series of frightened, keening yips.

A dog fight – and there was a time when on Saturday night and Sunday morning drunken men staggered along the street, when guns thundered with the sudden violence of death and the undertaker had another job. Over and done now. Frank gave credit again to Jed Stevens. Deadly with a Colt and seemingly fearless, what a lawman the man would have made! Too bad he and his deputy had taken the wrong trail.

Thought of Rance Bailey made Frank look toward the Geronimo. He saw several horses at the rack and remembered Yoder's statement that Bailey wore his gun tied down. Frank turned across the street.

Entering the saloon, he saw several men at the bar, their backs to him. One wore a heavy cartridge belt and Frank saw the Colt in the holster, thonged to the man's heavy leg. Frank's eyes lifted to the sign over the back mirror that repeated the warning against carrying guns.

Frank's lips flattened. A movement at the tables caught his attention. He was startled to see Dane over there, grinning as he listened to Cass Nolan.

The boy's presence jolted Frank, and angered him. The kid kept hanging around that drifter! But, more to the point, he would be watching Frank in case of trouble with Bailey. Frank didn't like that. As yet no one had seen him. He could take one step back through the batwings and call Rance Bailey at a better time. Frank's eyes cut to the broad back and rump. The holstered gun was a violation and Frank, the marshal, had seen it.

Frank walked to the bar and Dane looked up, startled. Nolan half turned in his chair. The three punchers at the bar saw Frank, and they eased away to the far end. The big man did not move or turn. He watched Frank in the back mirror.

Frank came up and the man turned, unconcerned. He was broad of shoulder and thick of chest. His round, dark face was tanned from the sun. The nose had been broken and the nostrils were broad. His lips were thick, and cruelty lurked in the corners of the mouth though he smiled now.

The eyes held Frank. Black and glinting, they hit with the impact of a mountain lion's, predatory and without mercy. Here was outlaw and devil, a savage in the dusty clothing of a chuckline rider. Frank could understand how, with this man, Jed Stevens had ruled the town with an iron hand.

Frank spoke levelly, 'You just rode in?'

'This time. Used to live here. I'm Rance Bailey.' A big finger flicked at Frank's badge. 'Used to wear one of those. Deputy, I was.'

'In town long?' Frank became aware of movement among the tables and he checked an impulse to throw a glance toward Dane.

'Waiting to meet a friend. Might be here a few days, maybe a long time.' The smile left Bailey's lips and he eased back. 'You've heard of me?'

'I have. Yuma prison – robbery – paroled.'

'That's right. I broke up a riot and saved the warden's useless neck. They set me free right then and there. That means I can go where I please and do what I please, don't it?'

'Not quite.' Frank indicated the sign above the bar. 'You've read that?'

'Sure. The damn' things are everywhere.'

'You're wearing a gun.'

'Ain't it so! I intend to keep on.'

'Then you'd better leave town.'

'Marshal, you ain't heard me good. I like this Colt right where it is. I like to be right where I am. No one takes the gun or orders me on.'

Showdown! Frank's gaze held steady, his face impassive. Inwardly, he went into turmoil. Where was Dane? Why did the kid have to be here? Bailey waited, having now moved back. There was a scurrying behind Frank as the bar hastily cleared.

'You're under arrest,' Frank said flatly.

'Now ain't that something! Think you can take me?'

Bailey's big hand hung just below the gun. Frank's Colt brushed the inside of his arm. His fingers slowly spread and he saw the lifting gleam in Bailey's eyes. The man was a killer!

Suddenly Frank wondered where Dane stood. The boy had never seen a gunfight before and, unknowingly, he might be in the line of fire. Frank's attention tried to hold two things at once – the killer before him and the safety of his brother.

In desperation, his head flicked to one side. Bailey moved. Frank knew he had made a mistake. Rance Bailey's hand slashed to his gun in a blurring move.

VI

Frank's hand slashed to his gun, lifting it from the holster as his thumb dogged back the hammer. He fell into a crouch, turning as the Colt cleared leather and his wrist twisted to bring it up into line.

He saw the black muzzle of Bailey's gun. It blossomed orange flame even as his own fingers tightened on the trigger. An iron fist struck his left chest. He fell, wondering why he should have lost control of his body. The room tilted crazily. In the instant just before darkness came, he wondered if Dane was safe.

He next became aware that a bright, rectangular form took shape, faded, cleared, resolved itself into a window. He had a body but, for the moment, he was detached from it. Then he felt pain centering on his chest.

He stared vacantly at flowered wallpaper, an ornate dresser with a big mirror. They were not his and this was not his house. Memory snapped back. This was not the Geronimo! Where was Bailey? Dane?

He tried to sit up. He gasped with pain and a hand touched him as his head fell back. Peg bent over him, her face drawn and concerned. 'Lie still, darling. Please!'

She moved aside as Doc Lakes' brown, leathery face appeared, topped by a shock of white hair. The man smiled but it did not quite reach his eyes.

'Too mean to die, Frank? But you will if you thrash around. You've lost a lot of blood and a whisper higher that slug would have smashed your shoulder.'

'What–?'

'Shut up. I'll talk.'

'But Dane?'

Peg appeared beside the doctor. 'He's downstairs, Frank, waiting.'

Peg disappeared again. Frank wearily closed his eyes. He felt deft fingers high on his left shoulder. He heard Lakes' voice as from a distance.

'Bailey shot you. He wouldn't let anyone move until he had a drink. He finally left the saloon. Your brother and a couple of others tried to help you.'

The voice faded, came again in mid-sentence. '...heard about it and ran over there. She made them bring you here and managed to check the bleeding until I came. Your shoulder will mend but the loss of blood worried me. I think it's stopped now.'

Again Lakes' voice drifted off, came back strong. '...build up strength. So you have to stay in bed. There–! I think it's safe to leave you for a while.'

Frank opened his eyes. Doc Lakes took a glass of water from Peg, opened his black bag and shook a pill out of a bottle. He returned to the bed, lifted Frank's head and forced him to swallow it.

'That'll keep you quiet.'

'Dane?' Frank asked.

Peg came up. 'He's downstairs, darling. He'll wait. Right now, you must sleep.'

Her face blurred as Frank drifted off. His mind asked, wonderingly, 'Bailey really beat me?'

It was night when he awoke. The lamp, turned low, shed a soft glow in the room. He turned his head and instantly Peg was at his side. He saw the marks of weariness in her face. 'You've slept a long time, Frank.'

He tried to move but winced and lay still, feeling the sweat break out on his forehead. 'Dane?'

'I'll get him.'

Peg left. Then Frank wondered what he could say to the boy. Dane had seen him go down. How could he explain it? Admit that Bailey was the fastest? Frank frowned. That wasn't true. If it had not been for that second he had looked away – but how could Frank tell the boy his presence had nearly caused his brother's death?

Maybe he could just pass it off with a wry joke about bad luck. But that wouldn't hold. Dane had seen the fight. He would think his brother grabbed at any straw to excuse his defeat.

The door opened and Frank slowly turned his head. Peg stood there, alone. 'He had to leave darling. I didn't know.'

He looked at her and she hurried on. 'Doc Lakes told him you'd be all right. His work … lot of it in the morning…'

Her voice trailed off. It was no good and she knew it. She could read his thought, for he could feel the heat of shame through the burn of fever. Dane had seen him downed by a secondrate hardcase like Rance Bailey. Dane was ashamed of his brother.

She impulsively knelt beside the bed. 'No, darling, don't believe it! You're making a mistake. Dane wouldn't–'

'Leave it be, Peg. It figures. I – can't blame him.'

'But…' She stopped and her hand sought

81

his. 'He'll be back first thing in the morning. Maybe tonight, when he tells Wills what happened. He'll want to be back.'

Frank managed a weary smile. 'Sure. You're tired, Peg. Get some sleep. I'll be all right.'

She slowly stood up and he forced himself to meet her searching gaze. She made a little twist of a smile and touched his hand again. 'I *am* tired. I'll be in the next room, the door open.'

'Why did you have me brought here?'

'To make sure you'd get good care.'

The next day Frank felt stronger but it was a false thing, as he discovered when he tried to sit up. Peg gave him food that was to help build up blood and Doc Lakes left pills for the same purpose after checking his wound and changing his bandage.

The day passed slowly, each hour Frank expecting to see Dane. But as the time passed into afternoon and waned toward night, Frank knew the boy would not come. A heaviness and pain in the heart added to that of the throbbing shoulder.

After supper, Peg sat with him. He heard the sounds of the town through the open window and then a movement at the door. His head jerked around eagerly but it was Owen Grange and Sol Burdick, calling to see how he was.

Not long after, Peg politely herded them out and then turned down the lamp. She came to the bed and kissed Frank. 'You'll be much better in the morning.'

'Peg, is someone watching the town?'

'Of course not! They know you'll be up and around in a short while.'

'But – Rance Bailey?'

'He hasn't shown up and isn't likely to.' She smoothed the covers. 'Frank, has this something to do with Jed?'

'Bailey knows Jed's out of prison, or near to it.'

'I see... Well, he also knows he was lucky – and nothing else.'

'No, he'll be back.'

'Sleep, darling! You fret and that'll do no good.'

At the end of the third day, Frank was impatient to be back on his job. He felt stronger and could walk slowly around the room. Doc Lakes checked his wound again and grunted when Frank demanded to know when he could return to his work.

'Your arm in a sling,' Doc Lakes said disgustedly, 'and you want to ramrod the law!'

'My right arm's fine.'

'Sure, untouched. Pretend you're making

a fast draw. Go ahead!'

Frank stared and then his hand slashed to his hip as he dropped into a crouch. Pain streaked along his left shoulder and into his chest, blinding him and leaving him gasping. He dropped onto the bed.

'See?' Doc said dryly. 'And you won't be able to walk more'n a block without wanting to rest.'

'Doc,' Frank said as the pain eased, 'I'm the marshal. I have to be around!'

'All right, Frank. Go to the office and just sit there a couple of days. Take a short walk now and then. But don't think you're going to do any real work.'

The next morning Peg worriedly watched Frank go down the steps and walk slowly away. He was aware that she looked after him. He held tightly to his determination and kept on, truly surprised that he tired so quickly.

His left arm felt a dead weight in the sling and his chest was sore and painful. He saw the grocer stop sweeping his walk and watch. Wondering if I'm any good, Frank thought, and then brought himself up. Naturally! after what had happened. So would all the town, including the Council. Frank had to find Bailey and have a showdown. It was that or turn in his badge.

He reached his office and leaned against one of the canopy posts to cover his need for support. He looked toward the Geronimo. The hitchrack was empty. No Rance Bailey, then, for the man would be certain to get his drinks at the Geronimo, his kind of saloon.

Frank went into his office, leaving the door open to relieve the smell of stale air and heat. He sat down behind his desk and closed his eyes. He thought of Dane and the twisting hurt returned. Damned if he'd let on to the boy!

He heard steps on the porch. His eyes snapped open and he sat erect, favoring his arm. Sam Yoder and Al Curran entered, stood diffidently just within the door until Frank waved them to seats. Yoder's sharp eyes touched the sling and then slid away. He cleared his throat. 'How do you feel?'

'A little stiff. Arm's sore. I'll be all right.'

Yoder worked his lips. 'That's fine, Frank. But until then ... maybe there's a good man who could be deputy?'

'I don't need one,' Frank said flatly.

'But you've taken a slug and you've lost blood! We know Stevens is on his way and Bailey's already here. They'll make a move for that money. A wounded lawman–'

'My gun arm's not hurt,' Frank snapped.

Yoder threw a glance at Curran, who fidgeted and then blurted, 'We have to be certain, Frank. You understand? Maybe if you had a deputy–' His face lighted. '–or called Sheriff Jensen from the county seat?'

A sheriff! A deputy! Frank could see either man downing Rance Bailey. If that happened, Frank could never redeem himself. Dane would always believe his brother had failed and so would the town.

'I can handle Apache Crossing. I intend to.' He let that sink in. 'Where's Bailey?'

'Out at Stevens' old place.'

'Give it a day or two and I'll go after him. I'll make it a personal score.'

Yoder rubbed his hand along his jaw. 'Bailey's fast with a Colt. No need to tell you.'

'But it–' Frank bit back the words. He couldn't say anything about Dane. 'But it will end another way this time.'

Yoder threw a glance at Curran and arose. 'Sure bound to – once your arm heals.'

The two men left Frank unhappily savoring their uncertainty. It must be infecting the whole town, but until he could move without pain slowing him up, he couldn't redeem his reputation. Now, he could only make the townspeople believe in him through his own air of confidence. He grimly set himself to the torturing task of making his rounds.

He slowly progressed from store to store from the Cattleman's to the Geronimo and finally to Manuel's *cantina*. Everywhere, he encountered a heartiness that concealed doubt.

The *cantina* was empty, except for Manuel behind the bar. When Frank entered, Manuel hastily pulled out a chair at one of the tables and then placed a shot glass of *aguardiente* before Frank. 'Drink it! It give you strength, *Senor.*'

Frank sipped at the raw stuff and immediately felt the burn and lift of it. He nodded thanks. 'Right now, I'm a damn' poor marshal.'

'Only for now. You must take care of yourself. The town has need of you.'

'Has it?'

'*Si!* Ah, it is this thing of the gunfight. The *ladron* had luck, Senor. No more! Luck is something that no man can say will be here or there. Should I not know? Look what happened to Ernesto. No, *Senor*, you will recover. Then this outlaw will have another kind of luck.'

Frank stood up. 'Manuel, you're better

than a dozen bottles of medicine.'

'You will be here a long time, *Senor*, guarding us.'

Frank left the *cantina* and made slow progress to the railroad station. He sat on a bench in the shade until the eastbound train arrived. He looked up in surprise when it stopped, for it generally thundered through.

A man descended, a carpetbag in his hand. The train sped away. The stranger stood on the platform, looking toward the town. Frank saw a slender, muscular man in his mid-forties with a hard jaw and firm lips topped by a thin mustache.

Frank saw, beneath the gray coat of an obviously new suit, the heavy buckle of a gun belt and the tip of a holster. Frank walked toward the man, who turned, catlike. The man's mustache was touched with gray and his eyes had golden flecks. They touched on Frank's face, flicked to the sling about the arm and the tip of the badge showing from beneath it.

He smiled and the narrow face became pleasant and warm. 'Is this a welcome, Marshal?'

'In a way. I–'

The man extended his hand. 'I'm Jed Stevens.'

Frank blinked but automatically accepted the hand. Stevens looked at the sling and then up at Frank, eyes dancing.

'Now when I was marshal, I figured a badge and a gun were enough to wear.'

VII

Frank's cheeks reddened. Jed Stevens appeared not to notice but Frank asked, irritation sharpening his voice, 'What do you intend to do in Apache Crossing?'

'It's my home, Marshal! Or it was – up to seven years ago.' His lips moved in a faint smile. 'I've been away, you know, at the request of the Territory.'

'I know. That's why I ask.'

Stevens looked down the dirt street to the corner where it bisected the main business thoroughfare. 'Same buildings. I suppose, the same stores. The town hasn't changed much?'

'Not much. A few people leave, a few come. Some die. Some stay away for a long time and folks wonder why they come back.'

'You make a heap out of nothing, Marshal. I'll look around. See who's come and who's gone. Sort of get the feel of the town again.'

'That shouldn't take long. And then?'

'Maybe a job, if I can find one.' His flecked eyes glanced at Frank's badge. 'I won't try for marshal, though I have experience – plenty of it.'

Frank liked this man and knew this was dangerous. Still, he grinned. 'Not for two years, anyway. Might try then.'

'Not a chance, even then. I might go to my old home. Again, I might pay a visit to my step-daughter. Peg still runs the hotel?'

'She does.'

'Right now,' Stevens picked up his carpet bag, 'I'll get a drink. That was a long and dusty train ride, friend.'

Frank checked him. 'You're wearing a gun.'

'Yes.'

'Now there's a change since you left. Guns are checked in. You get 'em back when you leave town.'

'How about the drink first?' He saw refusal in Frank's dark eyes and sighed. 'All right, I'll check the hardware right now.'

He unbuckled his belt and placed it in his carpetbag, the metal of the new gun glinting blue in the sun. He rebuttoned his coat. 'That satisfies the law, I reckon. Have a drink?'

'No, thanks. I'm making the rounds.'

'Another change. That never stopped me... By the way, my old house is still out there?'

'It's there, but changed by a hundred or so

hunters over the past seven years. Looking for stolen money. It's pretty well torn up.'

'But livable?'

'I guess so.'

Stevens' head cocked slightly to one side. 'You know, that's funny.'

'Funny?'

'They just couldn't believe the solid truth. I told 'em over and over I didn't steal that money. But they didn't believe it.'

'That's right, they didn't. Even your daughter can't be sure.'

Jed searched his face. 'How do you know? Has Peg told you?'

'Several times.'

'Well, now! That sounds real friendly.'

'Peg and I have been seeing one another. You'll find that out soon enough.'

Stevens' eyes became rock hard. 'In that case, Marshal, I'll go out to my home. I've had a bellyful of law and guards the last seven years.'

'You don't have to stay away from the hotel on my account. So long as you behave yourself, we won't have trouble. You're a free man so far as I'm concerned.'

Stevens smiled tightly. 'And you won't be watching me at all! No, thanks. I'll see Peg and then get as far away from you as I can.'

'Like I said it's up to you. Don't be surprised at the way the house and yard looks though. And don't be surprised to find a visitor out there.'

'Visitor? Another kind of lawman, I suppose.'

'Nope... Rance Bailey.'

'Rance! My old friend and deputy! Real touching he come all this way to see me when I get out of prison. Bailey used to be the meanest man I ever knew. Hot tempered and hellfast with a sixgun. Is he still that way?'

Frank's lips flattened. 'I've heard he is. But we're talking about you, Stevens.'

'Again?'

'Just keep within the law as long as you're in town.'

'Marshal, I intend to do just that – and loaf a lot.' His voice sharpened. 'You've taken my gun and warned me. You've told me about my old friend and that you and my stepdaughter are friendly.' Frank suddenly looked at a very dangerous man. 'Now, if you don't mind, I'll get that drink. I've picked up a bad taste. Then I'll go to the hotel and see Peg – again with your permission – and alone.'

'You're free to go and come. I won't bother you.'

93

'Friend, see that you don't.'

His eyes flashed and he bent to the carpetbag again. Frank watched him go. So that was the marshal who cleaned up Apache Crossing and then went to jail himself! Jed Stevens would not be a man to face in a gunfight and give odds you'd come out alive.

Frank heard a step and Sam Yoder came up beside him,. 'I was in the baggage room. I heard it all.'

They watched Stevens turn the far corner and disappear. Yoder thumbed his hat back from his forehead. 'Rance Bailey first – now him. It's started.'

He gave Frank's sling a long and significant look. Their eyes met briefly and in that second Frank read Yoder's open scepticism. But the Pinkerton man only nodded and stalked away.

Frank's eyes grew bleak and hard and he fought down anger. He knew what Yoder thought. If Rance could beat the marshal, what chance did the town lawman have against Stevens?

With a curse, Frank strode away. He went to his office, threw his hat on the desk and glowered at the cell block. Then, despite the heat, he closed the street door.

He worked the sling over his head as he

walked to the desk. He gingerly lowered his arm. It was stiff but he felt no pain. He worked the fingers and they responded, a bit slowly.

Frank turned to the closed street door. His right hand dropped to his side, just below his holstered gun. He waited a second and then made a blazing fast draw. The gun was no more than half out of leather when pain stabbed along his left shoulder and arm. For a split second, his movements almost halted. He levelled the gun and felt the waves of pain subside.

Very slowly, he holstered the weapon, dark face grim. That split second stop could have meant his death in a real gunfight. Frank picked up the sling and dropped it over his head, placed his aching left arm, into it. The pain subsided.

He inwardly cursed but realized the uselessness of it. Nature healed in her own time and not to man's schedule. Give it another day or so and Frank would see about Rance Bailey.

Frank opened the street door and looked toward the Geronimo. A man came out, walked a short distance to the saddlery shop and turned in. There was no other movement along the street and Frank wondered where

Stevens had gone. He wondered what the reaction of the town would be to the man's return.

He hitched at his gunbelt and walked to the Cattleman's. If he was any judge, Stevens would go there rather than the Geronimo. The Cattleman's was nearly empty. Two ranchers sat in huddled conference at a far table, there were three merchants at the bar, taking time from business for a quick drink. Stevens was not here. Frank turned to leave and saw Cass Nolan, alone at a table, nursing a drink while he worked a solitaire lay-out.

Frank's hurt and anger about Dane came to new life. Since the night of the shooting, Dane had not ridden in nor, apparently, bothered to inquire about him. Up to now, Frank had tried to excuse the callous absence. Dane was busy, maybe. He hadn't left until he knew his brother was not fatally or seriously wounded. So he would check in with Frank next weekend when the crew came in.

Now sight of Cass Nolan brought the whole thing up again. Frank felt that Nolan's influence led to Dane's neglect. It was an instinctive feeling. He looked across the room at the indifferent card player, angered, wanting to vent it and make things crystal clear to Nolan. Yet a strong urge to make sure before he spoke held him.

Just then, one of the men at the bar glanced up and saw him. 'Frank! Guess who was just here?'

The sudden interruption swung Frank back to the bar, aware that Nolan had looked up. The merchant raised a finger to order a drink for Frank as he came up. The other two made way for him and Frank saw they eagerly waited some comment.

'I know,' he said flatly. 'Jed Stevens. I met him at the railroad station.'

'What'd he have to say?'

'He wants to look around. Said he might go out to his old place.'

'You'd think he'd not want to show his face again!'

The second man said, 'I can figure why. If he hid that money, he's come back for it. Think that's it, Frank?'

'I don't know.'

'What are you going to do about him?'

'Now why does everyone think I have to ride herd on Jed Stevens? He served his sentence. He has a right to live here and come and go as he pleases.'

'I reckon he has. But it's kind of funny to

have Stevens and Bailey back in town. I remember how those two ramrodded Apache Crossing when they wore law badges. Cleaned the place up, I'll say that. But then they began to spread out. Took cuts from the saloons and even from Millie. Any gambler wanted to do business, he had to make arrangements with those two. You missed a bet there, Frank.'

'I never wanted that kind of money.'

'I will say, once Stevens and Bailey took the law badge, Apache Crossing became a safe town. Stevens and his deputy buried three gunslinging badmen and that changed things. The bad ones got the idea and, mostly, they stayed away. Those that didn't – they're buried now.'

'They had a good record,' Frank agreed flatly.

'Took some fancy gunfighting to do it,' the second man cut in. Frank caught his swift, slanting glance at the sling and his injured arm as he added, 'That's what we needed.'

Frank placed his shot glass on the bar, still half full. These men weighed his capability of ramrodding the law. He could tell them about Dane. But he knew that the statement of the truth would sound like an excuse. He'd show them in a few days in a way they could understand – Bailey in jail or with the other gunslingers in the cemetery.

He pushed away from the bar. 'Thanks, gents.'

'Hang around!'

Frank smiled bleakly. 'I have a job. Maybe later.'

He started to the door. Then he realized Cass Nolan watched him and had listened to the conversation. He looked at Frank as though he recognized evasion covering inability.

Frank felt the cynical impact, the concealed contempt. He swung sharply to the table, his dark face tight with anger. Nolan eased back in his chair. His glance touched the sling, lifted. 'How's the arm, Marshal?'

'It'll do.'

'Glad to hear it. Have a drink.'

'No. Seen Dane?'

'Not since...' Again the eyes cut to the sling. 'Seems like you're always hunting for him, Marshal.'

'Since he met you.'

'You're driving at something, Marshal.'

Frank indicated the scattered cards and the shot glass on the table. 'Gambling ... drinking ... that's something new for Dane. And a place like Millie's. All since you came to town from out of nowhere.'

Frank placed his hands on the edge of the table and leaned toward Nolan. 'I think you'd better leave the boy alone. Understand?'

He wheeled about. Nolan's voice lashed at him. 'Barton!'

Nolan's hard eyes travelled from his face to the law badge, half concealed by the sling. 'Where I come from is no one's business, Marshal. What I do and who I see is no one's business, either, so long as I'm within the law. So, that badge of yours don't count. I'll tell you this – I never talked Dane into a poker game, a drink or a woman. He's made up his own mind, like any man would.'

'He looks to you,' Frank said coldly.

'That's right. We're friends. I like the kid. You know, I think I'm the first friend he ever had he didn't come running to you to see if it was all right.'

Frank's lips opened, snapped shut. Nolan settled back in his chair. 'The kid comes around when he's in town. I treat him no different than I would any friend. I want to get drunk, I get drunk. If Dane wants to ride along, he decides for himself. I figure he leads his own life the way he wants to – like I do.'

100

Nolan's head hunched forward. 'I've broken no law. Until I do, keep out of my business. That's beyond a marshal's badge and you remember it.'

Their eyes locked. Frank spoke slowly. 'That's right – beyond the badge. But you remember, Dane's my kid brother. That makes it man to man between us if anything goes wrong.'

Frank turned and walked out of the saloon.

VIII

The evening sun sent long rays through the cottage windows and the first faint breeze from off the distant mountains stirred the curtains. Frank shaved slowly, stopping now and then to look thoughtfully at his reflection in the mirror. This was the first time that he had ever felt uncertain about supper with Peg.

Stevens was the cause, of course. He had gone to the hotel – and stayed. The whole town had eagerly followed his every move. And they couldn't wait to tell Frank, the marshal who courted the ex-outlaw's daughter. The town would watch just as eagerly tonight, make guesses and whisper.

Damned if he'd stay away, though. Peg would think that his first step in casting her off because Stevens had showed up. Peg would be certain that he considered his law badge more important than she. She'd have to know he didn't.

Frank wiped the lather from his smooth cheeks. He'd go. He'd show Peg – and the town – where he stood so far as Stevens was concerned. He paused again. Where did he stand? In the middle, holding off decision until he knew more about the man. He'd treat Stevens like any citizen so long as he behaved. He'd arrest him if he broke a law. That clear, he could dismiss Stevens now and try to make the best of the evening.

Frank carefully flexed his left arm. There were twinges up in the shoulder and Doc Lakes had said that the wound healed clean, and swiftly. Frank buttoned his new, clean shirt and glanced toward the kitchen clock. Plenty of time yet. His thoughts turned to Dane. He should ride out to Running W and see the boy. Forget his own hurt feelings under the circumstances.

He could try to re-establish the old relationship. Maybe he had been too harsh with Dane and had tried to run his life. Frank considered this and reluctantly decided he had been. This enabled Nolan to get to the boy.

Frank carefully creased his hat, flicked dust from the curling brim. Well, he could correct that. He'd see Dane and forget this older brother habit. Make it man to man, like Nolan had. Frank had absorbed too much of Maw's fear of the bad blood showing up. He could see that now. He'd watch Dane but not openly guide him.

Feeling better, Frank left the house. The sun had dropped below the mountains now leaving a soft blue sky shot with golden light. There was the first faint hint of purple shadows that the approaching night would bring.

Frank walked easily along the street. He could face Stevens now with confidence and he felt his new approach to Dane would be right. He approached the bank just as Owen Grange came out.

'Well, this is luck,' Owen said. 'I'd been hoping I'd see you.'

Frank waited for the banker to lock the solid doors for the night. Owen turned, weighing the big key in his hand. 'This is the first time in seven years I wonder if the lock is enough. Jed Stevens and Rance Bailey are too close for comfort.'

'They'll not be that foolish, Owen.'

'I suppose not.' Owen pocketed the key. 'Yoder said you met Stevens at the station and had a talk.'

'We did. Stevens knows where he stands.'

'Good!' But Owen's voice held the hint of doubt. 'Think you can handle him?'

'If it comes to that.'

'Of course.' Owen's eyes slid to the hotel and back again. 'Going to see Peg?'

'This is our regular supper night.'

'Yes … well, I thought… Jed Stevens is staying there.' Owen went on, purposely vague. 'I guess you'd expect that, seeing she's his daughter.'

'Step-daughter,' Frank corrected shortly.

'Yes, step-daughter.'

'Any reason why I shouldn't keep my date?'

Owen looked flustered, embarrassed. 'Why, Frank, I didn't say anything like that.'

'No, you didn't.' Frank adjusted his hat. 'The hotel is open to anybody who wants to stay there. I can't see any difference tonight.'

He smiled frostily at Owen, circled him and stalked off.

He crossed the street and mounted the steps to the hotel porch. He went back to the kitchen. Peg made a last minute check of the food with the Mexican women and she turned when Frank entered.

'Frank!' She came to him and gave him a brief kiss while the servants chuckled. She led the way to her own parlor. He had sensed a reserve in her kiss.

She closed the door and Frank came to her, arms out. She made a slight gesture that stopped him and he frowned. She involuntarily glanced toward the ceiling as though she saw someone in an upper room.

'You knew he's come,' she said.

'Yes, I met him.'

'Frank, he wanted a room.'

'What's wrong with that? This is a hotel.'

'But he won't say how long he'll stay.' She walked to a window and looked out on the deepening shadows. 'I'm glad he's come back and that he's out of that awful prison. I liked him before he left and, Frank, I still like him.'

'I know. You've told me.'

'I'm worried about him, Frank – and us. Mainly us.'

'Why?'

'Because he's living here. When you come to see me now, people will believe that you and Jed – well, you'll become friends. That's no good for you, Frank, wearing the badge. A marshal and an outlaw … well, maybe you'd better not come around. At least, until he's gone.'

Frank turned her about to face him. He looked deep in her eyes a moment and then swept her close and kissed her. She resisted a second and then her arms went about his shoulders.

'Frank,' she said in a soft whisper. 'I don't want Jed or anything to come between us.'

'It won't.'

'I don't want anything to hurt you. Jed could.'

'I won't let him.' He moved back. 'I've told Jed and all the others how I think. They all know. Maybe he'll go outlaw again, maybe he won't. That's not the point. He has a right to be here. You and me have a right to see one another. We'll leave it that way.'

'But what will the town–'

'I don't care about the town – just you. Now, how about supper?'

'Frank, Jed – he *is* my step-father. I–'

She broke off and indicated the little dining room through the archway. The table was set for three. He hid his disappointment that they would not be alone. 'Sure, Peg. What else could you do? And I know you wanted to.'

Her eyes glowed and she impulsively kissed him and fled for the kitchen. A moment later, Frank answered a tap on the door that led to the lobby. He opened it to face Jed Stevens, who quickly hid his start of surprise.

'Well, Marshal, I didn't expect you.'

'I told you how it was with Peg and me.

Right now, I'm not marshal.'

'That helps,' Jed said. As he walked by Frank, his flecked eyes strayed to the badge on the shirt pocket and there was a ghost of a smile on the lips beneath the trim mustache.

The meal was strained, though all of them tried to make it easy and light. Stevens spoke of the changes he had already noticed in the town, asked Peg about people, absorbed any scrap of news she could give him of events over the past seven years. He compared his problems as marshal with Frank's and was pleased when Frank said his job was lighter because of what Jed had done.

Then Jed's face grew pensive. 'Things sure change.' A wistful note in his voice disappeared under a cynical chuckle. 'Like tonight. It's the first time in seven years I've eaten with a lawman – as his equal.'

Peg hastily stood up, saying she had to check the service in the dining room. She left and Stevens produced cigars, offered one to Frank, who refused. Stevens carefully cut off the tip, savored the flavor. 'Peg has told me about you. Fine girl there.'

'The best!'

'Like my own blood daughter. Best thing ever come into my life.' Jed lit the cigar, covertly studying Frank through the flame. 'That's why I hope you and me can be friends.'

'I'm willing. One thing, though.'

'What?'

'Don't do something to make me a law-man. I can't be both at the same time.'

Stevens took a deep pull on his cigar and then considered the end. His gold flecked eyes lifted to Frank and a shadow of dis-appointment lurked in their depths. 'I reckon that's plain enough.'

'As plain as we can make it.'

Stevens smiled. 'Not that it'll ever come up. I don't like the climate at Yuma.'

Peg returned and, a few moments later, Stevens left, saying he hadn't as yet broken a seven year habit of early to bed. Frank and Peg went into the parlor and he again re-assured her. When he left to make his evening round, Peg clung to him a moment and then broke away with a smile.

'Darling, keep telling me nothing will happen. I so want to believe it!'

When Frank came out on the dark hotel porch, the red glow of the cigar marked Stevens' shadowy form. The man came toward Frank, stopped within the light streaming out the lobby door. He was not tall and yet he gave the impact of assured strength.

'Leaving, Marshal?'

'The rounds.'

'Yes, I'd almost forgotten. Long time since I've made them.' The cigar glowed ruby again. His eyes touched on Frank's left arm in the sling. 'I hear my old deputy's quite a hand with a gun. I didn't know he was that good.'

Frank sensed a deeper meaning under the words. It was in the tone, the way Stevens regarded him. There was the implication that Rance Bailey might be fast with a gun but he could be beaten. However, Frank was not the man to do it.

There was something even deeper. Frank sensed it in Jed's assurance. Stevens knew he could beat Bailey if it ever came to a showdown and he wanted Frank to know it.

Without words, Stevens had warned Frank to leave him alone.

IX

Frank said coldly, 'The business with Bailey's not over.'

'I didn't figure it was. One thing you can say for the town, it's never had a poor marshal – yet. Good night.'

He was gone, leaving Frank fuming. Stevens had warned Frank to walk carefully around him. He had also revealed his belief that Frank would not face Bailey again. If he did, he would lose.

Something like this must be going through the mind of everyone in town. The sling and the wounded arm were marks of Frank's defeat, all they could see. Frank moved the arm and inwardly cursed as the shoulder muscles pulled. How long would it take for the wound to heal? He had to meet Rance Bailey, and soon! Otherwise, he might as well turn in his badge before he was requested to do so.

He descended the steps and stalked along the dark street. His anger was still with him when he walked along the store buildings, approaching Manuel's *cantina*. He checked a rear door, the last along the block, throwing but a glance at the low, shadowy shape of the sun-warped wooden platform covering an old well.

He entered the *cantina* and saw that everything was quiet. He only nodded curtly at Manuel's greeting and left. He gave the dark main street a last, sweeping look and turned toward home.

Immersed in angry thoughts, it wasn't until he had turned in the walk that he realized a lamp glowed in the cottage. He stopped short. Who waited for him? He instinctively loosened the Colt in the holster as he strode to the door.

He saw Dane, and a pleased, surprised smile swept away the angry lines in his face. Then he saw Sam Yoder and Al Curran seated on the horsehair sofa across the room.

Frank sensed strain in Dane's angry mouth and in the questioning look he threw at Frank. Al Curran's beefy face was tight. Only Sam Yoder achieved a bland smile. 'Evening, Frank. We wanted to see you. Your brother let us in.'

Frank nodded, eyes cutting to Dane. 'Didn't expect to see you in town on a week night.'

Dane said with a touch of embarrassment, 'I figured it was time I come in.'

Yoder stood up. 'Frank, reckon we could talk now? It's important.'

Dane picked up his hat from the table beside the lamp. 'I'll leave.'

'No need,' Frank said quickly. 'You just rode in. Damned if you're going to ride right back again.' He asked Yoder, 'this won't take long?'

'Not long but … it's private.'

Frank nodded. 'Dane, how about making some coffee?'

Dane walked out of the room, closing the door behind him. Frank turned to the two detectives. 'Something's come up.'

'That's right,' Yoder answered. 'Al, you tell him.'

'Three men rode into town this afternoon. Happened I was looking out the bank window and spotted them.'

He stopped expectantly. Frank looked puzzled. 'What was special about them?'

'Bad ones. I run into them when I handled some train holdups east of El Paso. I was sure they were part of the outlaw bunch but I was never able to pin it on them. They operate along the Mexican border and deep into Sonora and Chihuahua.'

'Are they wanted in Arizona?'

'I don't know. Curly Blaine, Zack Meader and Lew Cross.'

Frank thought a moment and shook his head. 'I'm sure there's no dodgers out on them. They're clean here.'

Yoder said impatiently, 'I'm aware of that, Frank. Pinkerton gets all the dodgers.'

'Then?' Frank ignored the superior tone.

'We figure they're more buzzards after that stolen money.'

'Why?'

Yoder spoke with irritating patience, as though he explained something very obvious. 'Two masked men did the actual hold-up and robbed the express car. One was wounded when the guard sent a shot after them as they rode off with the money. He was found. But the other, Bix Terry, got away. We know he went to Mexico.'

'I know that.'

'Terry stayed in Mexico and he doesn't dare show his face up here. But I'll give odds Terry wants his share of that eighty thousand and he knew exactly when Stevens got out of prison. What's to prevent him from sending three of his outlaw pals – who are not wanted in Arizona – to see he gets his part of the loot?'

'Blaine, Meader and Cross?'

'Why not?'

'Well, for one thing, Terry in Mexico would be a fool to trust them. I never knew a renegade who wouldn't doublecross a friend for that amount of money.'

'Who said Terry was in Mexico?'

'You did.'

'I said he wouldn't show his face. He'd not ride into Apache Crossing where everyone knows him. But he could be hiding out beyond the town, close enough to watch his friends.'

'Well … that's possible.'

'It makes sense. Your jurisdiction ends at the town limits.' Yoder waited a moment and then added, 'Like you can't touch Rance Bailey.'

Frank's jaw tightened. 'What's this leading to?'

'I want to call in the sheriff, Frank. I don't want to do it behind your back, so I'm telling you now. Ike Jensen's authority extends over the whole county. You're limited.'

'Are you really saying you don't trust me?'

'Frank, I didn't say that. It just makes sense. You have to admit Rance Bailey downed you in a gunfight.'

'I'll even that score.'

'Will you? Bailey's fast. But let that go. Point is, you should've appointed a deputy, wounded as you are. But you won't. I understand why, but that doesn't change the situation.'

'A deputy marshal would be as limited as I am. So there's something else. What is it?'

Yoder hesitated but Frank's hard stare angered him and his expression revealed his basic dislike of Frank. 'I guess there is. I didn't want to say it, but you've forced it.'

'All right what is it?'

'That girl who runs the hotel. She's Stevens' stepdaughter and you're courting her. So, you might look the other way if she asked you to.'

Frank started forward but Yoder lifted his hand. 'I'm a detective, Frank. I make it my business to know what goes on – like tonight. You had supper with Stevens and his daughter. You know what Stevens is and what he plans to do. Still, you spend a real friendly evening with him. That's just too cozy for a lawman.'

'Stevens served his term, Sam. I have no right to arrest him or hound him. I'm courting Peg Winters. So it was my personal business tonight. But I'll handle Stevens if and when he breaks a law or goes for that money. I'll handle Rance Bailey when he comes into town. Understood?'

Yoder's jaw jutted out. 'We want Rance Bailey handled *wherever* he goes. You're not the man for it. I'm calling Ike Jensen.'

'Call the sheriff and be damned!'

The two men locked eyes, then Yoder snatched up his hat and growled at Curran. 'We've had our say. Let's leave.'

They went to the door. Yoder said in a choking voice, 'Nothing personal, Barton. I'm sorry it's working this way. But getting that money comes first.'

'Sure. But I'll still handle things in Apache Crossing.'

Yoder's lips pressed tightly. He jerked open the door and stalked out into the night. Curran eyed Frank, beefy face apologetic. Then he shrugged and followed Yoder, closing the door behind him.

Frank glared at the door, breathing deeply. He turned to se that Dane had come into the room from the kitchen. The boy's dark, lean face showed anger but there was shame in it, too.

Frank saw that the shame was for him. It shocked him that Dane felt this – for his own brother. Dane, of all people, should know him better! The shock deepened Frank's anger. He had been assaulted from too many directions.

Dane broke the silence, voice tight. 'They don't think you can handle Rance Bailey.'

'I can handle him!'

Dane's eyes were hurt and questioning. 'Then why do they want the sheriff?'

It was not really a question. Down under it was an appeal for Frank to say or do something that would preserve his stature, to give some indication of strength rather than of weakness.

Frank, in his anger, missed the appeal. He heard only the implied accusation. Bruised already, he heard only the doubt and his reaction was instinctive. 'Look, I said I'd handle Bailey. He's my business – not yours.'

Dane's young face flamed. His eyes glittered. He took a deep breath. Frank realized what he had done and started to speak. Dane cut him off.

'He's your business. Handle him – if you can!'

Before Frank could prevent, he strode to the door, flung it open and disappeared.

X

Morning sun streamed through the lace curtains of the hotel room and Jed Stevens looked down on the street. His eyes were distant, back seven years, as they slowly moved along the buildings across the thoroughfare.

They hadn't changed much, a new name replacing an old owner's here and there. His eyes lifted above the false fronts to the bare, sullen peaks of the distant mountains. He could see the dip of the railroad pass. Up there, Hy and Bix had held up the train.

Jed's eyes moved on and suddenly he thought of Millie. Good, sensible woman, Millie. No argument when he told her he wanted a cut of her business. She knew how it would be – arrests nightly until no one would come around.

The three saloons had all paid off. It had been a wild town then and they needed the marshal. Ah, good times! But penny ante. Let it go and no regret. A fortune waited, enough to buy a hotel like this ten times over.

That made him think of Peg. Seven years had given her a rich, mature beauty – made her look even more like her mother, that time he had met her in Lordsburg.

Thought of her made Jed grimace. Those stiff morals of hers! Still, a terrific woman and in love with him – at first, anyhow. A dozen times those scruples of hers had prevented him from making a killing.

He was glad that she had left him, but was sorry to have lost Peg, her daughter, not his. There had always been a strange sort of love between them, as though they were actually father and daughter. When her mother had died, Jed had come close to going to get Peg.

But she had written she would stay and nurse her stepfather. And that was the first Jed knew that after the divorce, his wife had married again. Lucky it happened that way, for Peg. Jed had ended up with seven years of prison. Peg's new father died and left her enough money to buy this hotel.

Jed shrugged. You never knew what turns the trail would take. Now, after all that, he was back with Peg. The old warmth was there but everything else had changed. A hell of a note, her about to marry a marshal!

Jed frowned out on the street. Right here, at this moment, he must make a final decision. He could make this hotel his home, he knew. Once everyone lost suspicion of him, he could get a job. It would be easy enough, for all he had to do was forget the money. Sooner or later people would think he had been innocent all along. He'd be fully accepted.

But he had served seven years of hell for it. Let eighty thousand dollars go by just to spend his life getting old and swapping lies in the Cattleman or the Geronimo! He snorted disdainfully and turned from the window.

He opened his carpetbag, took out the gun belt and holstered Colt. He donned coat and hat and left the room, carrying the gun belt looped across his forearm.

He went downstairs into the lobby, found it empty. Placing the gun belt and hat on a rack just outside the door, he went into the dining room. A Mexican woman placed breakfast before him and padded away.

Jed ate, mind busy with his plans. He had to know who watched him besides Rance Bailey. Once he knew – he grinned. He'd sucker them out of position, grab the money and be gone. Couldn't do that with Rance, of course. He'd stick too close.

Suddenly Marshal Barton, coming from the street, crossed the lobby without a glance into the dining room. Jed, cup of coffee poised, watched as Barton went to Peg's door and knocked.

Barton opened the door and a second later it closed behind him. Something in the marshal's face interested Jed. It was troubled, dark – and that could easily concern him.

Jed unhurriedly arose, crossed the lobby to Peg's door. Too bad, he thought, that Barton was too attached to duty and the badge to be bribed with money – or by Peg. Jed waited just before the door. He heard a faint murmur of voices. Unabashed, he placed his ear against the panel.

'More of them have come,' he faintly heard Barton say.

'Who?' Peg asked.

'Three renegades from Texas. Yoder thinks Bix Terry's hanging out close to town and he sent them in to make sure Jed has come.'

'Who knows about this?'

'Yoder and Curran.' Who in hell are they? Jed wondered and strained to hear more clearly. 'Owen Grange – and that means the town Council.'

'Frank, I know what the town must be thinking.'

'Now, Peg–'

'It's true, Frank. Everyone will ask if you'll close your eyes to Jed and the others because of me.'

'They know better.'

'But, Frank...'

Jed lost interest. Let them argue. He moved silently away, placed his hat on his head and looped the gun belt over his arm. He strolled out onto the porch and breathed deeply of the warm morning air. He moved down the steps with the air of a man who had nothing particular to do and plenty of time in which to do it.

He strolled by the Cattleman. So Bix Terry had shown up with unknown friends. There was Rance. How they all wanted to get their hands on that money! Jed's lips thinned under the trim mustache. He had not spent seven years in a hell hole just to split the loot several ways. There were too many of them gathering now, what with Bix and his friends showing up. Yoder and Curran – probably Pinkerton or railroad detectives – and within a week, Jed thought, the sheriff. He wondered if Ory Reid still wore the star and almost laughed aloud. Now there was a bumbler!

He turned in at the livery stable. In a few

moments he reappeared riding a hired, rangy bay, gun belt looped about the saddlehorn. Without so much as a backward glance, he rode to the edge of town.

Jed lifted the gun belt and strapped it about his waist. He touched the horse into an easy gait, still not looking back. But a subtle sense told him he was watched. He grinned. Let them!

The past flooded back. He recalled this turn in the road, that gully, that cluster of reddish, sun-baked rocks, the broken country lifting up to the gaunt, barren mountains.

At last he saw the paloverde trees and the house, low and squat against the high, rock-jagged curve of the hills immediately behind it. He kept to his slow and steady pace.

As he turned in the sandy road that led to the house, he drew rein. His flecked eyes travelled over the yard. Everywhere he saw the marks of ancient digging – and one or two that looked fairly recent. Scars showed about each tree, close to the house, all over the yard.

The house itself showed the effects of search, siding ripped off here and there, parts of the porch torn off. The place had almost been destroyed. He wondered how much the stable and outhouses had been torn up.

He rode to the house, eyes sharp on the dusty windows and the closed door. He came up before the porch, reined in. The door opened and Rance Bailey stepped out. For a long moment, Jed and his old partner silently studied one another.

Jed grinned. 'Rance, I never thought it possible. But you're uglier than ever.'

Bailey grinned in turn, shrugged. 'Yuma didn't pretty you up none, either. I been expecting you.'

'Well, now – I figured you'd be around.'

'Light and come in. It's your place but you're welcome.'

'Thanks,' Jed said dryly. 'I hear you're living here.'

'Camping is more like it. You'll have to make do with what I've got.'

Jed swung out of saddle and ground-tied the horse. He looked around the yard, a long and sweeping glance, then thumbed back his hat and stepped up on the porch. Bailey walked in ahead of him, leaving the door open.

Jed stepped into what had once been a pleasant room and stopped short with a spasm of anger and fury as he looked around.

Destructive gold seekers had added to the erosion of seven years' neglect. A fine horsehair sofa was now a rickety, bulging wreck of ripped covering, exposed and rusty springs, soiled and protruding wadding. The carpet was shredded. Wallpaper hung in strips where seekers had torn the walls to the studding in their search. The windows were thick with dirt so that only a suggestion of bright sunlight penetrated the room.

Bailey sat on a cot with rumpled blankets. He indicated a straightback chair that had once been in Jed's bedroom. 'Rest yourself. I got coffee making.'

He went into the kitchen. Jed crossed to the door and looked in. Here, again, was destruction, dust and dirt. Rance stood before a range that had once been a polished black. A coffee pot bubbled. A grimy table, holding tin plate and mug, stood under a window. Jed saw Bailey's food supplies on the shelves of a gaping cupboard. Bailey crossed to it, picked up a dust-grimed, thick china cup. 'They left a few things.'

'Damn' little!'

Jed came into the room. Bailey washed out the dusty mug in a pail of water, filled it and his tin cup with coffee and brought them to the table. He kicked out a chair for Jed, sat down himself. They sucked cautiously at the hot brew, covertly studying one another.

Rance broke the silence, after he followed Jed's frowning look a round the room. 'A lot of people hunted for that money. Everything's torn to hell and gone.'

Jed laughed harshly. 'And all for nothing.'

'I figured.'

Jed's shrug dismissed it. 'Hear you and the new Marshal tangled.'

'Nothing to it. You've seen his arm?'

'It's healing. He might come looking for you, Rance, figuring it was just luck.'

'He'll learn better.' Rance again looked about the room. 'Yeah, they sure hunted everywhere for that money.'

'It was never here.'

'Knowing you, I could've told 'em that. But we were both in prison.' He grinned. 'There's just two of us to divide it now, what with Hy dead and Bix ain't been heard of in years.'

Jed waited. Rance sipped at his coffee again and then impatiently banged the cup onto the table. 'How about it, Jed?'

'What?'

'The money. You know where it's hid. It's all over now and time to divide it. Let's do it right now and ride off.'

'It's not over. The banks and the railroad still want the money. They could be watching us.'

'What of it? We're here alone and no one's watching.'

'The money's not here.'

'Close?'

'Well ... yes. But we'd better be careful.' Jed covertly watched Bailey's coarse and impatient face. 'We've waited seven years – what's a few more days, or weeks?'

'Just that much longer, that's what. I want to get what's coming to me. You promised and, by God, you'll keep it!'

Jed sighed. 'All right, Rance. We run a risk. But if you want it–'

'I want it. I've waited too damned long now.'

Jed's fingers drummed on the table edge then he lifted his hands in a small gesture of surrender. 'Saddle up. We'll get it.'

'Is it far?'

'You sound like the gents who tore up this place. Let's find out.'

Shortly after, they rode away from the house, heading up the slope to the hills behind it. Jed rode a little ahead of Rance, whose heavy face was alight and eager. On the brow of the hill, Jed reined in and Rance made an impatient sound.

'Hold up,' Jed snapped. 'You want us both to lose out at the last minute? I'm making sure no one trails us.'

He looked back down the slope and over the barren range toward the town, afar off in the distance. He saw only the spread of high, crook-armed saquaro, the immense land and sky, the mountains dwarfed in the distance. Nothing moved that he could see but Jed did not believe it. He kept his thoughts to himself as he straightened in the saddle and lifted the reins.

'Nothing. It's a little further on.'

He led the way over the shoulder of the hill and down the far slope. They now rode in broken country, along a crooked draw that threaded the silent and forbidding hills. Jed's eyes cast ahead and to each side, now and then flicking at Bailey.

They made several turns and the hills fell back and they entered a small, barren valley. They had ridden about five miles now and Bailey revealed a slight edginess, though he said nothing. They rode the scant mile across the short valley and approached another shallow canyon. Jed saw what he wanted. He pointed to a huge, ugly, red rock.

'There.'

Bailey stared, eyes avid. Jed threw a swift look over his shoulder and thought he caught a flick of movement back across the valley. He sharply looked at Bailey.

'I buried it just under the rock on the far side.'

He unconcernedly urged the horse forward and Bailey followed. They rounded the huge rock and Jed drew rein, pointing to a volcanic irregularity in the stone.

'See how that finger sticks out, down toward the base? Right under it.'

He looked at Bailey. The man's heavy face had grown cold, his eyes hard and narrowed. His tongue moistened his thick lips.

'I know, Rance. It's the way you figured it. You want it all. Now that's a joke. So do I. Just one of us is going to leave here alive.'

Bailey jerked. Jed still smiled, but it was deadly and his flecked eyes glittered with a cold light. Bailey read the purpose in them. His heavy hand dropped to his gun.

Jed's hand moved with the blur and speed of a striking snake. The Colt whipped from the holster and a slight flick of his wrist brought the black muzzle up. His finger pressed the trigger as Bailey's Colt started to line. Jed's gun roared.

The black hole appeared in Bailey's forehead as his head jerked back with the impact of the bullet. His fingers opened spasmodically and the gun dropped as his big body fell to the ground. His limbs quivered a moment and then went slack. Jed looked at the body, making no attempt to calm Bailey's skittish horse. He ejected the spent cartridge and reloaded.

He holstered his gun and looked back across the valley. Nothing moved but Jed still had that feeling of watching eyes. If anyone watched, they would know Rance had made the first move to his gun.

Finally, Jed looked at the slack body of his one time partner. His lips pursed and he sadly shook his head.

'Rance, you were always slow witted. Did you think I'd hide it that careless?'

He lifted the reins, turned the horse and, swaying easily in the saddle, rode back toward the house and the town.

XI

Frank Barton stepped out on the porch of his office and pulled his hat brim low against the glare of the late afternoon sun. The day had been peaceful, except for one episode that still rankled.

Sam Yoder had reported that Jed Stevens had ridden out of town, gun belt wrapped around his saddlehorn. Yoder believed Jed rode to meet Rance Bailey.

'Al Curran's trailing him, since he's out of your jurisdiction and...'

His voice trailed off but Frank knew there was doubt he could handle Rance Bailey, let alone two of them if trouble brewed.

He grimaced now and pulled his hat brim lower with a savage tug. On such a peaceful day, he could limit this final round to the Geronimo and Perez'. And probably waste time, he growled beneath his breath.

As he started across the sun blasted street, he saw a rider coming in. He recognized Jed Stevens, who waved him to a halt. Frank waited until Jed rode up and drew rein.

'Afternoon, Marshal. You're just the man I was thinking about.'

'Why?'

'I rode out to my old ranch. You're right, they sure tore the place up. But the point is, I've been trailed the whole day. Your doings?'

'No.'

'Thought not. I don't know who it was, but I reckon you'll find out. They'll report a little trouble I had.'

Frank stiffened. 'What trouble?'

'An argument with Rance.' His voice grew plaintive. 'Ain't I to have a life of my own, Marshal? People watching and spying all the time. I wish they'd believe me. I had nothing to do with that robbery.'

'No one at the trial believed it. They sent you to prison. Why should they believe you now?'

'I guess I'll have to put up with it. But how long? I just want to live in peace. No need for folks to spy on me. I can't lead 'em to any money cache.'

'Or won't?'

'See there, Marshal! Even you.' He sighed. 'You know, I wish they'd found that money the night of the robbery. It caused hell's own trouble then and it can cause hell's own trouble now.'

'Then if you know where–'

Jed smiled wearily. 'I waste my breath. I can see that.'

He neck-reined his horse and rode to the livery stable. Frank looked after him, frowning, sensing something. He had noticed that Jed's gun belt was wrapped around the saddlehorn now that the man had returned to town.

Frank went on to the Geronimo and stood under the canopy, waiting. Jed came afoot out of the livery stable, the gun belt looped about his shoulder. Hat brim pulled to the sun, he walked to the hotel and disappeared. Frank rubbed his hand along his jaw, frowning, then shrugged and went into the Geronimo.

An hour or so later, Frank sat in his office looking out the open door on the street. He glanced up at the clock and decided to go home, bathe and change clothes for the evening. He stood up, reached for his hat and froze.

A heat bedraggled Al Curran rode up to the hitchrack. He led another horse, carrying a slack body, roped face down across the saddle. Frank swiftly circled the desk and strode out to the rack as Curran swung out of the saddle.

Curious men from the Geronimo strode across the street and more hurried up from the stores along the way. By the time Frank stood beside the body, at least a dozen curious townsfolk converged on him.

Frank lifted the uncovered head and looked at Rance Bailey's slack features. Shot between the eyes. Frank let the head drop and wheeled to Curran. 'Who done it?'

'Jed Stevens.'

'Stevens!'

'It was a fair fight. Rance lost. Maybe we'd better talk this over inside.'

Frank's eyes cut to the curious crowd. 'All right. Wait until I take care of this.'

Curran went into the office and closed the door. Frank brushed aside questions as he pushed through the ring, leading the horse bearing the body down the street to the barber, who was also the undertaker.

Some of the curious trailed along. Frank helped the barber take Rance into the big back room and then led the horse to the livery sable. He warded off ghoulish curiosity and returned to the office. He grimly thought as he crossed the porch that the town was well rid of Rance Bailey. He only wished that he had been able to do it himself. Then he opened the door and stepped inside.

Yoder had joined Curran and now sat with troubled face on a chair near the wall. Curran had been talking to him and turned when Frank entered. Frank closed the door behind him.

'What happened?'

'I trailed Jed Stevens out to his ranch,' Curran said, 'keeping out of sight.'

'But he knew it. When he came in, he told me he had been trailed.'

Curran said defiantly, 'I did the best I could. That's open country.'

Yoder cut in, 'Frank, did Jed tell you about Rance?'

'He said I'd hear about a little trouble he had. Let's hear your story, Al.'

'Jed rode to his place and Rance Bailey came out. They talked awhile and went inside. I couldn't hear anything but they looked friendly enough. I hung around until they came out again.'

Curran glanced at Yoder and continued. 'Both of them rode into the hills. I had to wait until they were out of sight and then followed. I went slow, trailing. I didn't want to show myself. Then I saw them in a little valley, maybe five miles or so from the house. They were by a big rock. That's when it happened.'

'Fair fight you said?' Frank said.

'Rance drew first. I had glasses on 'em and I saw that. Stevens was just one hell of a lot faster than Bailey. I'd hate to face him.'

Yoder's eyes rested on Frank in unspoken doubt. Frank flushed, getting the implication. What chance did he have against Stevens?

'Did Jed really know he was trailed?' Al insisted.

'He did. I told you.'

'Anyhow, he never got off his horse. Just reloaded his gun and rode back my way. I had to skip around the hill and wait until he was gone. Then I rode to Bailey. Nothing I could do there, so I picked up Jed's trail. Sign was clear for a long time and then – like that! – he shook me off.'

'Jed knows the country,' Frank said. 'You don't. I hear in the old days he could throw an Apache off his scent.'

'Now what chance did I have! Anyhow, I went back to Bailey, worked him across his horse and brought him in.'

Yoder stirred. 'One thing worries me about this. Jed shook Al off. It's pretty clear he didn't do it because of Bailey. I say he did it so he could get to the buried loot, dig it up and bring it in.'

Frank shook his head. 'No sign of it when I saw him.'

'Saddlebags?'

'Why, yes. But that money would make a big bundle. There was nothing like that.'

'He's been at the hotel a long time since you saw him?'

'That's right.'

'How does this sound, Barton? Stevens shakes Al off. He gets the loot and hides it at the edge of town, or maybe even behind the hotel. Then he makes a circle and rides in bold as brass. He goes to the hotel. Since you saw him last, he'd have plenty of time to get that money up to his room.'

Frank looked at Al. 'Where did he throw you off? About what time?'

Al considered, then described the place where the trail vanished and the approximate time. Frank turned to Yoder. 'I know this country. I'd say Stevens rode directly into town. He didn't have time for anything else.'

'I hope so!' Curran breathed. 'If he's got that money, we can depend on one of two things. He'll try to slip us and vanish. Or – there's Bix Terry and his gunhawks. They could try to get the loot from him. Either way, we lose.'

Yoder grated, 'We can't watch 'em all.'

'We're guessing he has the money,' Frank said reasonably.

'Damn it! I'll bet on it!' Yoder came to his feet. 'That money belongs to the banks and not to a bunch of renegades. Right now Stevens has it. I wish to hell I had the authority to arrest and search. I want the county sheriff!'

Frank managed to hold his temper. 'Stevens is in town. I have authority here equal to the sheriff.'

'Well, then?' Yoder demanded.

'What right have I to search, except your suspicion?'

'Then a lot of good–'

Frank cut in, 'But if you issue a complaint, I can act. I'll go to the hotel and find out.'

Yoder grunted, hesitated. He studied Frank. 'How about Stevens? He could be dangerous. Have you thought of that? He beat Rance Bailey and Bailey was fast enough to down you.'

Frank said tightly. 'You won't believe me, but that was a fluke. Maybe I'll explain it later.'

'All right,' Yoder conceded with no real

conviction. 'Even so, Stevens always was fast – and now he's on the other side of a law badge.'

'How about the search?' Frank asked coldly. 'Do you want it made?'

Yoder and Curran exchanged glances. Yoder said slowly, 'I'd like it, yes.'

'Then you're asking me, representing the banks and the railroad, to search Stevens' room? You believe the money's in his possession?'

Yoder understood the question. Frank, as marshal, put it officially. Yoder nodded. Frank hitched at his gun belt. 'That's all I need. Since you're the complaining parties, do you want to go with me?'

Again the two detectives exchanged glances and Curran's held a glint of uncertainty. He moistened his lips and nodded. Yoder gestured toward the door leading to the street. 'Lead on, Marshal. We'll go with you.'

As Frank started out, Yoder checked him. 'Marshal, we've no authority here. If we want someone arrested, we always have to go to the local law.'

'I know that.'

'Just to keep things straight, Marshal. You'll have to handle Jed Stevens and make the search.'

Frank's dark, level eyes rested on Yoder for a long moment. Then, without a word, he strode out on the porch and turned toward the hotel. Yoder and Curran followed a step or two behind.

XII

Frank climbed the steps to the hotel verandah and walked across it to the open main door. Peg moved across the lobby to the dining room but stopped short when she saw Frank and the two men behind him.

'Frank! Is something wrong?'

'Nothing, Peg. Is Jed here?'

She threw a glance at Yoder and Curran, back at Frank. 'Up in his room.'

'Has he left it since he came in earlier this afternoon?'

'I don't think so. I've been busy, of course, but I think I'd have known if he had.'

Frank asked Yoder, 'Still want to?'

'She doesn't know. She just thinks,' Yoder said heavily.

'Frank, what is wrong?'

He smiled. 'We just want to talk to Stevens.'

She stepped aside as Frank turned to the stairs. He walked down a narrow hall to the front of the building. As he rapped on Stevens' closed door, he saw Peg back at the head of the stairs.

The door opened. Jed Stevens was in his shirt sleeves, collar open, unarmed. His hair was rumpled and Frank saw the marks on the bed where he had been sleeping. Jed looked at Frank and then at the others. 'Well, Marshal, I've been expecting you.'

'Why?'

'About Rance.' Jed's flecked eyes showed faint amusement. 'Which of these gents trailed me?'

Curran looked confused and Frank had a wry, secret pleasure introducing him and Yoder. Jed gravely nodded to each in turn. 'More to this visit than Bailey?'

'Maybe we'd better talk inside.'

Jed waved them in. Frank walked into the small room. Jed's gun belt, the Colt in the holster, hung from the back of a chair over in a corner. Jed entered behind them, closing the door. 'If it's about Bailey—'

'And a little more,' Frank cut in. 'I want to search your room.'

'Why? On what authority?'

'These gentlemen think you have the stolen money. They've made a formal complaint to me.'

Stevens looked from Yoder to Curran and then back to Frank. He sighed. 'I reckon I'll have to get used to this. Go ahead.'

He leaned against the doorjamb as Frank searched. He paid no attention to the marshal but to the two men, with a faint glint of triumph far back in his eyes. He now had two more enemies identified.

Frank knew, from the moment he began, the search would be fruitless. Stevens had made just the right amount of injured complaint, and his complete indifference as he leaned against the door was sure sign of it.

Nonetheless, Frank made a thorough search, as much for the two detectives as anything else. They'd have no reason to charge him with carelessness. Yoder and Curran watched as he opened luggage, tore up the bed, examined the closet. Now and then they looked uncomfortably at Stevens, who ignored them. At last Frank finished.

Stevens straightened and asked thinly, 'That all Marshal?'

'Not quite all. Now we get to Rance Bailey.'

Stevens shook his head, looking down at the floor. 'Who'd have thought Rance and me would tangle, close as we were in the old days?'

'But you did,' Frank said dryly. 'What have you got to say about it?'

Jed looked at Curran with faint amusement. 'This one saw it all. He trailed me. He can tell you it was a fair fight. Rance drew first.'

'We know that. I'm not arresting you. Bailey's death is no loss.'

'I don't like to think of Rance that way, even though I did it. It was self defense.'

Frank looked sharply at him, hearing near-laughter in the sad voice. He saw nothing but a mock sorrow that he had to accept.

'What caused the fight?'

'An argument.'

'About what?'

'Marshal, I'm not going to answer that. It was personal and Rance got mad. He tried to draw and I beat him. It was witnessed.'

Frank looked to Curran, who slowly nodded. Frank made a small gesture. 'Then we have no further business here.'

Jed, lips pursed and eyes suddenly hard and direct, moved over to the chair. As Frank's hand touched the doorknob, Jed said, 'Marshal, just a minute.'

'Yes?'

'Let's all play our cards face up. You made a search on the complaint of these two. You found nothing. You know Rance drew first and you've let that drop. Right?'

'That's right.'

'Then you've no business in this room again. You've no right to bother me here, out in the street, wherever I go unless I break a law. That goes for these two snoops.'

He stood close to the chair and his voice grew harsh and tight. 'You can take this how you want it – a warning, a threat, whatever. I want to be left alone. I've got the means to be left alone.'

His hand blurred to the handle of the Colt in the holster. Frank's hand slashed to his holster and even as the gun flashed up, he saw that Jed had checked the move of his own hand. By then, Frank's Colt had levelled on him.

Jed slowly lifted his gold-flecked eyes to Frank. He grinned. 'You're fast, mighty fast. It's something to know. Now I wonder how come Rance beat you.'

Frank realized his left shoulder had given only a slight twinge, not enough to impair his draw. Yoder and Curran stared at him and then at Jed, whose hand had fallen away from the looped gun belt. Yoder's eyes narrowed and doubt sprang anew in them. After all, Stevens actually had not tried to touch his gun.

Frank sensed that the play had been a deliberate test of his own gun speed. Jed had

146

coolly taken a certain risk in the experiment. Now the man knew, and Frank gave him credit for brains and courage. He holstered his gun.

'Sorry.'

'Don't be,' Jed said, and moved away from the chair. His voice grew cold again. 'I figured sooner or later I'd get a visit like this. You had one search coming. Well you've had it. You know I don't have that money.'

'Not yet,' Yoder blurted.

Stevens' glance flicked to him, back to Frank. 'Now I'm going to cut cards my way. Leave me alone. This goes for all of you. The next time I'll be wearing a gun or be close to one. I always was good with a Colt. I still am.'

'Don't wear it in town,' Frank warned evenly.

'Of course not, Marshal. I've read those nice big signs and I'll obey the law. But there's another one on my side – self defense and protecting your property. Don't forget it. I won't.'

He moved around them to the door and opened it. He bowed with mock politeness. 'Now, gents, if you'll leave me to my own business, I'll leave you to yours.'

Frank walked out, hearing Yoder and

Curran behind him. The door closed. Peg still stood at the head of the stairs, face drawn and frightened. She started toward Frank, a question on her lips. He took her arm and, with a slight frown warning her to silence, walked her down the stairs to the lobby. He turned to Yoder and Curran.

'Satisfied?'

'No,' Yoder growled, 'but we have to be.'

Frank jerked his head toward the stairs and Stevens' room. 'Stay out of his way. He has the right of the law.'

Yoder stalked out the door, Curran following. Frank watched them disappear down the street. Peg touched his arm.

'Frank, what was that all about?'

He knew he must tell her. He indicated the departing detectives. 'They thought Jed had the stolen money. They figured he'd slipped it into his room today. I didn't believe it, but they wanted a search. He didn't have it.'

She glanced toward the stairway. 'I heard Rance Bailey has been killed. Has this something to do with that? Jed did it?'

'It was self defense. Al Curran saw it. There's no charge against Jed.'

She considered this, hand still on his arm. She spoke slowly. 'If Jed met Rance, it was for a purpose. That means he's actually guilty, Frank. He was in on that robbery. He knows where the money's hidden. Maybe he and Bailey had an argument over it.'

'Jed says they had a quarrel. You could be right, Peg. But you could be mighty wrong, too.'

'No, it has to be!'

'Does it? Figure it this way. Jed rode out to his old place and that's natural enough. Bailey's out there and, remember, he confessed he had the money, claimed he passed it to Jed, who hid it. Jed's denied that all along. Maybe Jed was jailed because Bailey lied and Jed tried to force the truth from him and it ended in a gunfight.'

'Do you believe that, Frank?'

'It could have happened. On the other hand, it could be just the way you called it. We don't know – yet.'

'What can you do?'

'Watch him, but at the same time figure he's innocent until he proves he's not. The law works that way. We'll know which it is sooner or later.'

Her fingers tightened on his arm and she suddenly kissed him. He smiled. 'Now what was that for?'

'For thanks. For being fair. More than that,

for honestly telling me everything about Jed. A lot of people will say you're giving Jed every chance because of me. They'll say you'll–'

'Peg! We've been over that.'

'All right, Frank.' After a moment, she said, 'Then you'll just wait. I understand that. But you must be careful.'

'I think I can meet anything that comes up.'

'Jed could always handle a gun. He's downed some of the best gunslingers and now Rance Bailey.'

Slow anger formed in his eyes. 'And Bailey beat me. Is that it?'

'Frank, I'm just saying–'

'Can I stand up to Stevens? Will I, after what happened to Bailey? The rest of the town must be asking that, too.' He smiled bitterly. 'Well, all of you will have to wait until it happens. Then you'll know.'

His anger blinding him to Peg's stricken face, he strode away. He heard her call after him but he walked on, half running down the steps and the street, dark face harsh.

By the time he dropped into the chair behind the desk in his office, his anger lessened. He leaned back then, looking vacantly out on the street as he weighed the reason for his anger.

He should not have cut Peg off. He had to admit that, from what she knew, her fear for him was justified. He could tell her about Dane, but he still felt that the truth would sound like an excuse. So all she knew was that Bailey's slug had come within a whisper of killing him.

His own knowledge of what she and the town must think made him touchy. But he could only wait until the moment came when Frank could prove once for all...

It hit then, shocked, turned him cold. Why hadn't he seen it before? Because of Yoder and Curran and the search of Stevens' room, because of his anger at Peg. But it had been there from the moment Curran came in with that beefy body across the saddle.

Frank could only redeem himself in the eyes of the town by facing and downing the man who had shot him. But today, Jed Stevens had killed Rance Bailey. That removed forever any chance of another showdown. From now on, people would only know that Bailey had bested their marshal. Their lawman had failed. They would ask but one question.

Since Frank had been beaten by a second-rate gunman, what could he do against Jed

Stevens if the man broke a law or went for that hidden loot?

They'd all be asking – the town, Owen Grange, the Council, Yoder, Curran – all of them. Even Peg – and Dane. Frank's face tightened as the full implication of the situation hit him. They'd wonder now – all of them – if he'd have a chance against *any* gunhawk who came along.

Frank's reputation as a lawman, his stature in the eyes of Peg and Dane, was at stake.

And the path to redemption through Bailey was closed.

XIII

Dane Barton sat in the comparative cool of the big barn, where now and then the air stirred through the wide doors, touching his scowling, lean face.

He repaired harness, a necessary task. His wide hat brim was pushed back from a tanned face, so much like Frank's, though not fully fleshed out. He looked up from his work, eyes squinting against the blazing light streaming through the door. He occasionally heard a lift of voices from the two men who worked out of sight back in the stalls. Dane scowled with a gnawing sense of injury when now and then he heard a laugh or a whistle from the two who worked where heat lay trapped in nearly suffocating layers.

Perhaps Lew Wills' inadvertant remark had done it. He had given Dane the harness job, saying the youngest and newest of the crew could handle it, not knowing that the words cut into Dane's pride.

Actually, the incident was only sympathetic. Dane had been withdrawn and smart-

153

ing ever since his angry exchange with his brother that night the two detectives had come to the house. It had been bad enough when Frank had been downed by that saddlebum, Bailey, right before Dane's eyes.

He hadn't believed it. Frank had lost stature. He wasn't the tall man that he had led Dane to believe. For days Dane had been ready to fight the first man who made any belittling allusion to the fight. Dane had hoped something would be said so that he could vent anger and chagrin through his fists.

The crew had left him alone and it galled Dane. For the first time in his life, he had met with a problem that had no easy solution. He couldn't beat it down with his fists, he couldn't shape it in his mind because anger, wounded pride and reflected shame interfered. He couldn't talk about it and yet he wanted to. He could only simmer in futile anger.

So, he had become even more withdrawn. His emotional wounds were too raw to expose, even to Cass Nolan let alone the men in the bunkhouse. Silence built a wall around Dane behind which he suffered alone.

It gnawed at him now. He heard the two in the back of the barn and wondered what in hell made them so happy. He heard Jim's dry crackle and then Bronc's heavy, youthful voice came clearly.

'I wonder if the Marshal ever caught up with Bailey.'

'No matter he will,' Jim answered. 'I know Frank. He ain't one to back down.'

'Ain't you right!' Bronc answered with a crowing laugh. 'But he can sure *lay* down.'

'Bronc! My God, the kid's—'

Dane stormed in. Bronc made a placating gesture. 'Hell, kid, I didn't mean it. A bad joke, that's all.'

Dane strode straight to the taller, heavier man. Bronc's square-jawed, earnest face tightened. 'Kid, I said I'm sorry.'

Dane's fist caught Bronc high on the cheek. The force of it sent Bronc momentarily off balance and Dane bored in. Flaming anger streaked through him and a flooding sense of joyful release. At least there was something physical he could strike.

Dane's fist slammed into Bronc's mouth, bringing a trickle of blood. The sting of the blow erased Bronc's thoughts of apology. He warded off another blow and then his mauling fist slammed into Dane's stomach. The boy doubled over, only to be straightened by a hard, lifting blow that caught him on the chin. Dane had a split-second sensation of bursting lights.

Then he sensed foggy movement and felt that some exterior force propelled him along. Gradually the lights began to acquire substance. He became aware that men held him, though he was seated on something.

His eyes focussed. He sat on a chair in the bunkhouse. Water dripped from his hair. His jaw felt broken and his stomach was a massive ache. He looked blankly up into Jim's deep seamed, leathery face. Dane looked around. Jim, Bronc, and the ranch cook hovered about him. Bronc heaved a deep, contrite sigh.

'Kid, I sure didn't want to do it, but there was no stopping you.' Dane glared sickly and Bronc tried again. 'I shot off my mouth. I didn't mean your brother was—'

'Shut up!'

'Leave him be,' Jim said.

Bronc walked out, followed by the cook, at Jim's slight signal. Dane sat with lowered head, fighting nausea. He gingerly touched his jaw.

'Feel better, kid?' Jim asked.

'Good enough to ride out.'

'What you want to do that for? Bronc's apologised and wants to forget it.'

'Did he forget my brother!'

'Kid, we know how you feel. You've been proud of Frank. I heard about that fight. Something happened–'

'It happened. Rance Bailey shot him and then walked off as big as you please. I was there. I saw it. It's all over town and the whole range. Even Bronc–'

'Dane, listen to reason!'

Dane came to his feet, stood a moment until the dizziness passed. Then he walked to his bunk and made up his roll, Jim watching in distress. Dane straightened, his possessions packed. Jim looked so miserable that Dane grudgingly relented.

'Not your fault, Jim. Mine – for losing, like my brother. And both fights fair. The Barton brothers ain't much of a size.'

He walked out.

Riding out of Running W, Dane felt a sudden let down. What the hell had he done, cutting out like this? His jaw set again. He couldn't stay after Bronc had beat him. Like his brother, Dane had lost something of his size.

He faced the problem of the immediate future. He didn't want to go to Apache Crossing. Even if he didn't stay at the house, he'd meet Frank on the street, in a store.

Frank would look him up, once he heard the news. Explaining what had happened and why was a little too much at the moment. Dane thought of Cass Nolan, living at the edge of town. It would be the one place where Frank wouldn't come.

Dane cut off the road, making a beeline to the place Cass Nolan had rented. He was still some distance away when he saw three men come out of the house, mount horses and ride off.

Dane looked after them. He had not clearly seen their faces but he had the impression of rawhide strength – and something he couldn't quite define. But it wasn't pleasant.

However, his own troubles pressed. He turned in at Nolan's yard, swung out of the saddle and walked to the door. It opened and Nolan's heavy bulk filled the dark frame. His heavy face showed surprise and a trace of uneasiness.

'What brought you to town?'

'I quit.'

'What happened?'

'Just quit. Ain't I welcome, Cass?'

Nolan caught himself. 'Sure, Dane, sure. Come in.'

The front room was sparsely furnished and Cass had not added a stick of his own since he had rented the house. Dane dropped his roll just inside the door, skimmed his hat to a bare table and dropped into a chair, feeling the heat and his aching jaw. Nolan moved slowly from the door.

'I thought Running W had a permanent brand on your behind.'

'Not me. I got tired of being stuck way out there.'

Cass dropped into a chair, beads of sweat standing on his high, florid forehead. The trace of uneasiness still showed in his sharp gaze. 'That ain't the whole story.'

Dane suddenly knew he could talk to Cass and tell him every little damn' thing – about Frank, and himself, and the fight, and quitting. The words gushed out.

Cass listened, full lips pursing now and then. He sat with big hands hanging over his knees, heavy head lowered a little and thrust forward. Dane finished and Cass went into the kitchen, Dane looking worriedly after him. He sensed disapproval and that bothered him. Cass returned with a bottle and a couple of glasses.

'I'm drinking. How about you?'

Dane accepted the shot glass. He took it all in a single gulp. His eyes filled with tears and his breath caught. But it went down and the whiskey eased his aching stomach. Cass returned to his chair and spoke at last.

'Sounds to me like a damn' fool thing. But I suppose you had to stick up for your brother.'

'It was more for me than Frank. It was like they run me down, though it was Frank they talked about. If it wasn't for that... Frank and me ain't exactly friends now, let alone brothers. You know that.'

'I've seen it. I wonder why.'

The whiskey working, Dane angrily blurted all the reasons, every irritation, instance of control, disagreement and strain into a satisfying bill of complaint.

'And besides,' Dane ended, 'I'm damned tired of him running my life. I can think for myself and work for myself. I figure I can take care of myself.'

'So do I. Now you've quit, what do you want to do?'

'I don't know. I have to think it out. Might stay around Apache Crossing, might go and see what's on the other side of the mountains. I thought ... maybe ... I could bed down with you for a day or two.'

Cass carefully considered Dane, his uneasiness replaced by some new idea. He asked at last, 'Got a wandering?'

'Something. I don't want to stick around the Crossing, that's sure. But I don't know what else.'

'Well, I might think of something. But first, I want to know dead certain whether you're going to ride your own trail or your brother's.'

Dane started to answer but Nolan's up-lifted palm checked him. 'You've just been in a fight, rode off your job and you're mad. That's no time to think clear and straight, something you have to do if I'm to help you.'

He picked up the bottle, crossed to Dane and refilled his glass. 'You're welcome here – leastways until you've got it all lined out.'

By suppertime, Dane's anger was almost gone. He had moved in by the simple means of throwing his roll on a bed in a small room down the hall. For the first time, he felt free and unchecked in the way of his life, like a man should.

Nolan asked Dane if he wanted to go along to the Geronimo. Dane refused, honestly stating he didn't want to meet his brother just yet.

'Dodging him?'

'Not permanent. Just not ready for showdown yet.'

After Nolan left, Dane blew out the hot

lamp and sat in the darkness of the front yard. He looked at the lights down the street toward the heart of town. He heard a distant, soft laugh and suddenly felt very young and alone. He wished he had gone with Cass.

The big man came home early to find Dane still in the chair, tilted back against the house. Cass eased himself down in the doorway, looked out in the night a long moment.

'Rance Bailey was gunned down today.'

The chair legs made a dull thud as Dane jerked upright. 'Frank?'

'Nope. Fellow named Jed Stevens. It was a fair fight. Happened outside town.' Cass yawned loudly. 'Wonder what your brother thinks now.'

'Why?'

'Bailey downed. Bailey was a better man with a Colt but he didn't look very good to me. Yet he beat your brother. With what happened today, Frank's on his way out as a lawman. Who can be sure of a marshal who goes down with a slug from a wandering hardcase like Bailey.'

Dane said faintly. 'I heard Bailey was good.'

'Maybe once. But I can judge a man and

162

I've got an idea about your brother. It's not only mine. I heard it at the Geronimo tonight. He talked a gunspeed he didn't have – maybe never had. He fooled the town for all these years and then got showed up.'

The silence grew tense. Cass broke it, voice softer. 'Sorry, Dane, but that's the way the talk's going. You ought to know.'

'Sure, Cass.'

The big man yawned again and stood up. 'I reckon it's cooled off enough to sleep. Turning in?'

'After a while.'

Nolan left him, his crooked smile hidden by the darkness.

For a long time Dane remained outside, turning the information and its implications over in his mind. Then he finally went to bed. He stripped and lay staring up at the ceiling, feeling the sweat ooze from his naked body.

He thought of Frank and tried to figure him out – and their life together, clean back to when Maw had died. Dane had always respected Frank and obeyed him without question up to ... when? About a year ago, maybe longer. Why then? Had Frank changed, or had he?

Frank hadn't. Frank always directed his

163

life, Dane thought. When he was a kid, it was all right – making him go to school, come in from play, study, wash his neck and ears, buy his clothes, tell him what to eat, teach him things about riding and shooting. A kid growing up needed that, like he needed a home. Frank had done that.

But Dane was a grown man now and still Frank tried to tell him what to do. He tried to force a stern, uncompromising code on Dane. Good in its way, Dane admitted, but some of it didn't yet make sense. Frank shoved it all down his throat. Same way, Frank picked his friends – admitting some, chasing others away. What did he say? 'All wrong' – that was it. Nothing else.

No, Frank had not changed. Dane had. He thought man now, and acted man – most times. The night at Millie's with that little blonde. He knew for sure then. Of course, he should've stopped drinking and the rest wouldn't have happened. And Frank had jailed him! – his own brother! That still rankled.

Take Cass Nolan. Dane liked him. Something free and easy about the big man, like no place could hold him for long. He rode his own trail in his own way. He was the first to accept Dane as a man.

But Frank raised hell! Hinted to Dane that the man was close to outlaw and even half-way threatened Cass. Nolan had told Dane.

He viciously punched his sodden pillow. To hell with Frank! Cass was right. He had to ride his own trail. Then doubts came. For all Frank's faults, he'd never told Dane wrong – about anything. In his way, Frank cared. Dane sighed and tossed, a badly confused young man. He had to see things straight, but he couldn't. Still troubled, he drifted off to restless sleep.

Nor did morning bring a decision. He and Cass had breakfast and Dane washed up the dishes while Cass went out to the little barn behind the house. Dane had finished the last plate when he heard a knock at the front door. He hurried to open it.

Frank stood there, worry lines in his lean face and an unconcealed anger in his eyes. 'I heard you were here.'

Dane nodded, too surprised to answer. He just stood in the doorway.

'I met Lew Wills at the Cattleman's. He told me about your fight. Said you quit.'

Dane caught his speech. 'That's right.'

'Why didn't you come home?'

Dane instinctively bristled. He couldn't really explain and that made him angry and baffled. 'I didn't want to.'

'I see. You'd rather live here instead of where you belong.'

Dane heard a sound. Frank's eyes jumped to someone behind him. Dane turned. Cass had come from the barn. His square, hard face looked like granite and he swept Dane aside. He faced Frank. Dane felt the immediate crackling animosity between them.

'What are you doing here, Barton?'

'I've come for my brother.'

'Did he ask you?'

'No.'

'Then I reckon Dane can make up his own mind.'

'He's coming with me, Nolan.'

Their eyes locked, then Cass looked at Dane, who saw that the decision rested on what he had to do in the next few minutes.

'You want to leave, Dane?'

Dane took a deep breath, shifted his weight back and forth and then shook his head.

'There's your answer, Barton,' Cass said. 'Now you get the hell out of here and off this property. That law badge gives you no privileges.'

Dane looked miserable but he could not back down. Frank's face paled. Cass grinned as he looked at the gun in Frank's holster.

'Only your Colt can buy you anything here. After Rance Bailey, even that don't mean much.'

Dane flinched. Frank's eyes blazed in fury and his fists clenched. Dane knew the signs. Cass had pushed too far. Then, in amazement, Dane watched the fighting anger brought under control, the clenched fists opened, the wiry body swayed back from the door. Frank looked at him.

'Your home's waiting, Dane. Do you want to come?'

Frank showed every sign of backing down. It left Dane speechless but through his amazement, anger and shame arose.

'No!' he blurted.

Frank turned on his heel and strode to the street, where his saddled horse waited. Dane swayed toward him and then caught Cass watching. Out in the street, Frank swung into saddle, neck-reined the horse and rode off, stiff and, Dane felt, beaten. Something heavy and ugly knotted in Dane's stomach. Unreasonably, he felt abandoned and hurt because of it. Cass grunted and Dane's eyes slowly turned to him.

'Forget him. He backed down. You're smart to cut loose. He'll always back down.'

XIV

That night, the meal in Peg's apartment was strained. Frank's anger at Dane had not left and Peg had sensed his mood from the moment he came in the lobby. She had looked sharply then her eyes deepened and she had silently opened the door to her rooms and admitted him. She closed the door and kissed him. 'You're tired. It's been an all-wrong day?'

He nodded and she led the way to the small dining room. She said nothing as they ate but watched him with concern and worry. Normally, she spoke of the small incidents of the day over coffee, but tonight she said nothing. She cleared the table and joined him in the front room. She sat down beside him on the sofa and her small hand felt warm and comforting in his.

'Is it anything I can know?' she finally asked.

He told her then. He had learned of Dane's fight and of his quitting the Running W. Later someone had reported seeing the boy at Nolan's after Frank had waited most of the day for him at the office or at home. He told how he had gone to Nolan's and of what had happened.

'So he turned me down,' he finished bitterly 'for someone who can only lead him into trouble.'

He subsided into dark thoughts, staring across the room. Peg sat quite still, her hand still in his. Frank stirred restlessly, grimaced.

'Nolan had the right of it out there. It's his place. He could order me off since I wasn't there on law business. Once he told me to leave, I was trespassing.'

Peg stirred but said nothing and Frank was grateful for her understanding. 'I could leave or fight. I'd have been wrong from the beginning if I'd started trouble. Nolan, damn him, knew that. All I could do was ride off.'

He jumped to his feet, paced across the room, whirled to face her. 'Dane – he must think I'm a coward!'

'He probably does.'

His jaw dropped and he stared. She hurried on before he could protest. 'Every boy looks up to someone, Frank. He makes a hero, because he needs one. Most of the time it's a father. With Dane, it's an older brother.'

'Then why–'

'Listen, darling, please! I know how you feel, but see it from his side. You've done a good job raising him but you've been pretty stern.'

'Strict,' Frank corrected.

'That, yes – and stern. I've seen it now and then. I think you'd be the last to claim it, but you can sometimes give people a feeling you're always right.'

'Peg! You know that's not–'

'True? I know. If you weren't human, darling, I wouldn't love you. Probably Dane has had that feeling more than anyone. Up to now, you've been an anchor for him, someone he could look up to, someone he could be proud of.'

'Up to now!' Frank repeated bitterly. 'He's sure changed his mind in the last year.'

'He's growing up. There comes a time when every boy wants to step out of his father's shadow and cast one of his own. It's normal. He's restless to get away from the family. It doesn't mean he's stopped loving them but that he has to set out on his own. You've been Dane's family – all of it. He's just following the pattern.'

Frank thoughtfully sat down beside her again. She was right. He could remember some of this himself, except that Maw's need had held him close to her and his job. Then his jaw hardened. 'He only had to say he wanted to have a little freedom.'

'I think he did,' she answered gently, 'but not in words. He began to find friends of his own.'

'Cass Nolan! There's something wrong with the man–'

'Frank,' she cut in and placed her hand on his arm, 'he had to find out for himself. You never gave him the chance.'

He subsided again. She was right in one way, he admitted. But he couldn't sit around and watch the kid get in trouble. Cass Nolan brought back the incident of the morning and his anger stirred again.

'Why do you say Dane thinks I'm a coward?'

She said slowly, 'In some ways, boys are like girls. We worship our mothers and then, one day, we find out they're something a little less than holy. They're women. It shocks us.'

She turned intently to him. 'What happens when a boy's hero changes into just an ordinary man? If he shows a single human

weakness, or fails at something – like everyone does – what happens?'

'Well ... shouldn't the kid expect it?'

'He should, but he doesn't. No hero has
flaws. He's not a hero anymore. The boy
goes the other way. His hero becomes a
coward. Actually, he has been neither – only
a man, strong some ways, weak another.'

Frank leaned forward, hands on his knees,
frowning at the red, rose design carpet. She
gave him an understanding glance. 'Most
kids gradually learn the truth about their
heroes. It's not so bad that way. I think that
was happening to Dane. It would have
worked out except for – Rance Bailey. He saw
it, Frank. It was a hard blow.'

He moved uncomfortably and she saw the
momentary anger lines about his mouth.
Then he sighed and told her what had happened – of his fear Dane was in the line of
fire and how Bailey had used that split-
second advantage. She listened in amazement and her eyes glowed at Frank with
admiration.

'Why haven't you told this before?'

'Think it over,' he answered harshly. 'It
sounds like a sick excuse. I figured I'd meet
Bailey again and even the score. But–'

'Jed killed him,' she finished. 'You never

had the chance. But, why didn't you tell Dane?'

'It'd sound even worse to him. After what happened this morning, he wouldn't even listen.'

Peg knew he was right. She bit at her lip. 'I guess you can't. But, darling, let Dane stay with Nolan.'

'What else can I do?'

'At least understand him – try to. Let him grow up on his own and make his own mistakes. They won't be bad. I'm sure of that. Why not tell him you *want* him to handle his own affairs?'

The old thought and habit pattern made him swing around. 'And let him grow wild – and maybe outlaw?'

'I know, Frank. That's always bothered you. But maybe you're seeing the bad uncle in Dane when he's not there at all. Can't you see he has a lot of you in him? It's there, far more than the uncle.'

'I don't know... I just don't know.'

'Try it. Give him a chance.'

When Frank left the hotel, Peg's kiss still warm upon his lips, his mind was in a turmoil. She made sense, he admitted. She had seen a lot more things than he had. Yet he couldn't be sure. What would she think if she saw Dane's sulky eyes and the angry curl of his lips so like his uncle's? These were sign certain. Maw knew, she had worried. But maybe even she had been wrong.

He sighed and, needing relief, pushed the problems to the back of his mind. He'd tackle them again after he had made his rounds. He turned into the Cattleman, found it in dignified peace as usual. He chatted a few moments with the bartender and some patrons, then left.

He sauntered down the dark walk along the line of closed stores to the Geronimo. He pushed through the batwings to find it nearly deserted. Only four men stood at the long bar, a scant half dozen tables were filled – the mid-week doldrums. His sweeping gaze checked abruptly at one of the tables.

Dane and Cass sat there, a bottle and glasses before them. Frank's nostrils flared and he nearly walked out. But the sight of the two – and the whiskey – was too much. He deliberately walked to them. They looked up and Dane half rose, settled back. Nolan's heavy face set in lines of mocking challenge.

Frank stopped at the table. They faced him, like enemies, even Dane. That cut and

174

it angered him, but he held it in check. He had come to a decision in that moment of seeing Dane and it has strengthened as he walked to the table. It was almost as if, deep in his head, he could hear Peg's soft, understanding voice. But he faced Dane with a defiance of his own.

'Dane, you want to cut loose.'

Nolan spoke lazily, 'Sure he does. So why don't you leave the kid alone?'

Frank's eyes merely cut to him, back to his brother. 'You got a right to live as a man, on your own, in your own way.'

Dane's eyes rounded and his mouth dropped. Frank's voice tightened. 'So you can make up your own mind and ride your own trail. This don't mean I'm turning my back on you, but it does mean that I'm not horning in any more.'

Even Cass Nolan sat in silent surprise. Frank took a deep breath. 'I'll say just one thing. Men live by rules and law. Abide by them and you'll be all right. Break 'em and you're in trouble. Understand?'

Dane numbly nodded. Frank bored on, determined. 'That's the way it'll be. You can depend on it. So, if you want to stay at the house, you can. If you want to stay somewhere else – with people like Nolan – that's up to you. I won't argue.'

Frank started away, then wheeled around to face Nolan. He studied the surprised man for a long moment and then spoke tightly.

'Treat the boy right – if he chooses you. If you don't, I'll come after you – and not as a lawman. That's a promise.'

He turned on his heel and strode out, leaving Nolan and Dane to stare after him.

XV

The small house seemed empty and lonely to Frank. The rooms, small as they were, echoed to his steps. It was Dane, he knew, and that was the strange part. When Dane had worked at the Running W, the house had been empty like this from one week-end to the other. But it hadn't echoed. It was Dane's home then. Now, the boy had made his choice and he was not here. That made it empty.

Dane remained at Nolan's. It worried Frank but he tried to keep his mind off it. Peg was right, leave him alone. She said he would soon come around, and Frank had to believe that for he had already made too many mistakes in handling Dane. It was hard, the waiting, the uncertainty.

So now, he only glanced in at the Geronimo, not wanting to meet Dane or Nolan, not wanting Dane to feel his older brother watched him. Frank spent more time in the Cattleman and, for relief, with Manuel Perez.

Manuel was easy to take. Frank liked him, though he became irritated now and then when Manuel mourned Ernesto with deep sighs and rolling eyes. After seven years, a man should begin to recover, Frank thought. But, then, who could tell about these emotional Mexicans?

Despite himself, Frank became interested in that long ago killing. At odd moments he'd wonder who the killer was and he'd try to solve the case even at this distance in time. It served to keep his mind off Dane.

Like this afternoon. He didn't feel like going to the office or to that empty house. Instead, he wandered into the alley and along it to the old well. The high, ancient curbing was long since gone. Only a low, wooden platform covered it, the wood curling slightly with sun and the years.

Frank leaned against a wall and looked back toward the *cantina*. On that long ago night, drunken Ernesto had weaved along this way. He came to the well and someone had attacked him. Another Mexican? drunk, or perhaps jealous of Ernesto's prowess with the dark-eyed *senoritas?* It must have been quite a fight, since the old wooden curbing had been broken and, judging from Ernesto's picture, he had approached Manuel in size.

Frank grunted, annoyed with himself. Why bother with an old killing, one nobody cared about except Manuel? He walked aimlessly back to the mouth of the alley. As he turned the corner of the building onto the street, he walked into Jed Stevens. They were both startled. Stevens looked back the way Frank had come.

'Marshal, you do a better job than I ever did if you check the alleys.'

'Just in case someone leaves a back door unlocked.'

'This time of day, no thief would take a chance.'

'Part of the routine,' Frank answered shortly.

'Sorry, Marshal. Every man handles a job differently. Let me buy you a drink. How about Manuel's?'

Frank saw no reason to refuse. He entered the *cantina* with Jed. At the sight of them, Manuel's eyes widened and he jumped up.

'*Senor* Stevens! You have been back long time and not come to see me.'

'My fault, Manuel. Besides, I didn't know how you'd feel about me.'

'Hey! What you mean?' He followed Stevens' glance to his brother's picture. '*Senor*, you do what you can that night. This

179

other thing...'

Manuel shrugged acceptance of fate. He poured drinks, refused pay. Stevens lifted his glass to Frank. 'Your health and luck, Marshal. May none of your troubles grow as big as mine did.'

'Thanks.' Frank drank.

Jed placed his empty glass on the bar and studied Ernesto's dark face in the frame. 'Now there was my one real failure as Marshal. Things happened too fast. Ernesto got killed – beside the old well up that alley by the way. I had no more than looked around when I was called to chase train robbers.'

He grinned crookedly. 'Who, according to a jury, turned out to be me and my deputy. So I never got back to Ernesto. I suppose they never found who killed him?'

Frank shook his head and Manuel heaved a sigh. Stevens signalled for a refill. 'At least one good thing came out of it for the town. I ordered that danger spot boarded up and it was done the next day. By the way, is the platform still there?'

'Getting old and warped but it's there.'

Stevens again lifted his glass, this time in a mocking salute. 'My sole monument, and I imagine it's rotten. Be best if the thing was filled up.'

'The cover's still solid.'

Stevens pushed away from the bar. 'Well, Marshal, good to talk to you again. I can see why Peg likes you. *'Dias*, Manuel.'

''*Dias*, *Senor*. And you come back, eh?'

Stevens smiled, flecked eyes warming. He waved a negligent hand and left. Frank walked after him to the door and watched the man stroll around the far corner. Manuel stirred at the bar.

'A good man, *Senor*. You and he are alike.'

'What!'

'But, *si!* Both of you speak to me like I am Manuel, not a greasy Mex. That is something, Senor, in this country.'

The days passed in a vacuum. Now and then Frank had word about Dane. He was often with Nolan at the Geronimo. The few times he and Frank met, there was a brief, strained exchange of words. Frank sensed the boy went through a period of decision and he must be patient.

Wait for Dane to decide. Wait for Stevens to make some move. Wait with Yoder and Curran, who waited and watched Frank with uncertainty and distrust. So, Frank thought grimly, the town must wait for another sign that its lawman should be replaced. Wait – but there was nothing else to be done.

Stevens remained in the hotel. He rode out to his torn up ranch once more for a brief visit. Yoder, who had trailed this time, disgustedly reported that Stevens had only strolled about the yard, looking at the buildings and then had come back to town. Later, Owen Grange reported the man asked if the place could be sold but then dropped the matter. Stevens loafed in the saloons, walked aimlessly here and there, cautiously renewed old friendships.

A week later, Frank sat in his office in the dragging hours of a hot afternoon. He half dozed. A man rode up to the hitchrack. Frank's feet hit the floor with a thud. He was at the door by the time his visitor stepped upon the porch.

'Well, Sheriff, I didn't expect to see you.'

Ike Jensen, square, affable face moist with sweat, grinned under his big mustache and he stretched the kinks out of his back and legs. He was a large man, verging on the stout.

'Howdy, Frank. I ain't been in this part of the county in a coon's age. You folks must think you ain't got a sheriff. I thought I'd show my ugly face.'

'Glad you did. Come in.'

Ike took his hat from his bald head and beat

travel dust from his clothing. He sank into a chair and sighed with relief. His shrewd, brown eyes moved swiftly about the small office.

'Office neat, jail empty, town peaceful. Looks like you've got a lawman's heaven.'

'Hardly. There's been a little trouble.'

'So I heard. Word come Jed Stevens returned, and some of the old robbery gang. Could shape up to a mighty mean tangle.'

'It could… Who told you?'

'I just heard.'

'Ike, you're too honest to run a false brand. I'll bet you've heard from Sam Yoder or Al Curran.'

Ike's pleasant face reddened. 'All right, I did. They wanted me down here and wrote you'd been touchy.'

'What else did they write?'

'About Rance Bailey. He downed you?'

'He did,' Frank said shortly.

'Faster with a gun?'

'No.'

'Then what?'

'Something made me look aside a second. That was enough.'

Ike sank deeper in the chair, studying Frank. 'That's all I need to know about it. I'm satisfied.'

'Thanks. You're the first.'

'That figures. I can just about guess what the town thinks.' Ike touched his star. 'I never could figure why people think a man with a badge is God, or something. Need help?'

'No! Not in the town. The county's yours.'

'I hear Bailey was killed.'

'That's right – by Stevens.'

'His old side-kick. Too bad. You should've done it.'

'The wound stiffened me for a while. Stevens beat me to it.'

'Why does bad luck run in bunches? Well, I reckon it's over.'

'It is.'

Ike squinted out the door onto the hot street. 'Sixty miles home in all this heat. Reckon it'll cool off?'

'Might, in a few days.'

'I'm getting old. I have to rest up before I hit the trail again. Damn' near roasted me coming down.'

Frank's jaw subtly tightened in anger but he suppressed it. Heat did not hold Ike Jensen. Uncertainty about the strength of the law in Apache Crossing did. But there was nothing Frank could do. He pulled himself from his chair. 'Welcome to stay at my place, such as it is.'

'That's neighbourly, Frank. Thanks. But I can't put you out. I ain't used the county's expense money in a month of Sundays. I'll stay at the hotel or with Owen Grange. Last time I was here I promised him.'

Frank shrugged, accepting.

That evening, Frank learned from Peg that Ike had not registered with her she had seen him talking to the banker. After the meal, Frank started his rounds, going first to the Cattleman, then the other saloons. All was quiet and he returned to his office until the late evening round. Time passed slowly but at last Frank, with relief, moved out into the street again.

He crossed to the Geronimo and pushed through the bat wings. A bunch of cowboys working the range near the town had come in and the saloon had an unusual amount of business. Frank moved slowly to the bar.

He glanced around the tables and saw Dane. The boy's dark face was flushed, his eyes bright and his gestures wide. He sat with Nolan and three strangers, hard looking men who grinned at Dane and then exchanged knowing winks between them.

Frank walked to the table. The three men grew subtly tense and their eyes narrowed.

Frank felt the impact of their instant dislike and wondered briefly if it was directed at him or his badge. He dismissed them, eying Dane.

'How's it been?' he asked. In that instant, he realized the boy was drunk.

Dane made another wide gesture. 'How's it been? Fine, big brother! Mighty dandy!'

Frank's cold glance cut to Nolan who sat unmoving with a glint of sly triumph far back in slate blue eyes. Frank bit back anger. 'Glad to hear it, Dane. See you soon.'

He strode away. He had to force himself to the bat wings and outside. He stalked across the street to his office. In the dark shadows of the porch, he waited, watching the Geronimo, fighting an impulse to go back there and drag Dane out. This time, if he had to check Dane's drunken antics, the kid would get the full treatment – fine and all.

But less than half an hour later, Dane came out with Nolan and the three strangers. They rode off in the direction of Nolan's house. Frank, relieved, hitched at his gunbelt and walked home.

He had a late coffee, lingering over it. Then he yawned, thinking of bed. A fist pounded frantically on his door. Frank crossed the room and threw the door open. Light streamed out on the dark, frightened face of the Mexican swamper from the hotel.

'Juan!'

'*Senor*, come quick! *Senorita* Peg–'

'She hurt?'

'She want you. At the hotel.'

Frank snatched his hat from the table, blew out the lamp and hurried along the street after Juan. Lights streamed peacefully from the saloons and there was an air of slumber about the hotel. But Frank bounded up the steps and crossed the porch with a clutch of foreboding.

He plunged into the lobby. Peg sat on a chair near the desk. Her hair had fallen about her shoulders and her dress was rumpled. She rubbed red marks on her arms and she jumped up when Frank entered, flew across the room and into his arms.

He held her, letting her sob away her fright. She clung to him, fingers digging deep into his arms. He smoothed her hair a moment and then held her at arm's length.

'You're all right?'

She nodded, sobs catching in her throat. She took a deep breath, gained a certain control though fright still showed in her face. 'Jed! Frank, they took Jed!'

'Tell me about it – all of it.'

'I heard noises out here and came out just in time to glimpse men at the head of the stairs. I didn't see their faces, then. I told myself they visited one of my guests but I was nervous. But I went back to my room.'

She held her face in her hands and looked up at Frank. 'Something bothered me. When I heard steps on the stairs, I had to come out – just to make sure. They were coming down then and they had Jed. He was hanging limp between two of them.'

'Killed? Knocked out?'

'Knocked out, I'm certain. I couldn't move. Then Cass Nolan–'

'Nolan!'

She nodded. 'He was down the stairs before I could move or scream, Frank. He grabbed me, put his hand over my mouth. I tried to break loose. Then one of the other men grabbed me. They pushed me out into the kitchen. The back door was open and I saw their horses out there in the light. They tied me up and shoved me in a closet. I heard them drag Jed across the room. Then I heard the horses as they rode off.'

She began to cry again and grabbed his hand, held it tightly. 'I couldn't scream. I thought I'd suffocate. But I finally worked loose and ran out. I sent Juan for you.'

Her face blanched. 'Frank! They've kidnapped Jed! What are they doing to him?'

'We'll get them – and Jed. They won't hurt him.'

'But why, Frank? Why!'

'There's just one answer – stolen money. I knew there was something wrong with Nolan! Bix Terry's waiting somewhere close and Nolan must be his friend. God! how he fooled us! Been here for months.'

'But, Jed?' she cried.

'I guess they got tired of waiting for him to go for the loot. They've grabbed him – maybe to force him to tell them where it is.'

He felt her stiffen with a new fright. He hurried on, voice soothing now with a confidence he really didn't feel. 'It's all right, Peg. They won't get far. I'll find them. They won't dare hurt Stevens.'

Her fingers tightened into his flesh and her wide, violet eyes looked up at him with a new horror. Words came in a choked whisper. 'Frank! When they pushed me across the kitchen, the light streamed out the back door and I saw their horses.'

'Sssh, it's over now.'

'Frank! Listen! The one who held the horses – it was Dane!'

XVI

Frank's body grew cold and his mind became numb for a moment. He saw Dane, earlier at the Geronimo, drunk, with Nolan and the three hard-eyed strangers. They must have been the men Peg had seen carrying Stevens. He could picture the boy holding the horses.

Frank had warned Nolan and the man had laughed. No wonder, an outlaw friend of the hiding Bix Terry! Frank's face contorted with fury. He wheeled about. Juan, the swamper, was gone. Juan probably babbled about this kidnapping right now at the Geronimo, or Manuel's. At least he did not now about Dane. Perhaps Frank could reach the boy before Ike Jensen—

He heard a muffled shout from the rear of the building. Frank raced to the kitchen, across it and through the open door. His Colt was in his hand, hammer dogged back, as he plunged into the yard and halted, adjusting to the night shadows.

'*Senor!*' Juan called. 'Over here!'

190

Frank moved swiftly in the direction of the voice. He saw a man crouched over another sprawled upon the ground. Juan's voice shook. 'He is dead, I think.'

Frank knelt beside the Mexican. He fumbled a match from his pocket and struck it. The brief flame revealed the starring, sightless eyes and white, slack face of Al Curran. The match went out and, swearing, Frank struck another. He saw the dark spread of blood on Curran's shirt. Frank bent forward as the small flame flickered. Stabbed! The match went out.

'*Senor?*' Juan wailed the question.

Frank raced away down the dark alley. He could think only of Dane. Murder, and the boy implicated! He couldn't believe it. There had to be something more than Stevens' kidnapping to explain this. He had to find Dane – fast.

The thought of Ike Jensen in town made Frank run the faster. Dane faced a hang-noose unless Frank could reach him, get the truth. Dane! The thought of his brother erased all logic. Frank knew only the grim necessity of reaching him before anyone else did.

He plunged into the small, dark stable be-hind his house. He did not need a light, his hands reaching surely for the saddle, swinging it onto the back of his horse. He raced into the house, came out a moment later carrying a rifle in a leather scabbard.

Frank cut off the main street and rode a circuitous route to the edge of town. He drifted down the street, past houses where lamps glowed peacefully. Nolan's was the last along the street, a few yards beyond the town limits. Not a light showed but Frank felt certain that beyond those dark walls Nolan and the hardcases held Dane as well as Stevens prisoner. The kid just wouldn't voluntarily be a part of this. Wild, maybe – but not outlaw!

Closer now and there was still no sign of life, no light. Frank swung out of saddle and lifted his Colt from the holster. He drifted forward to the house, eyes darting to the shadowy corners, the blacker rectangles that marked lightless windows. He expected a movement or challenge at any tense second.

None came. Frank now stood within the very shadow of the structure. His ears strained for muffled sound and his eyes probed into the darkness. He came to the doorway, stopped. He cautiously extended his hand and gripped the doorknob, turned and suddenly slammed it back, throwing himself to one side, clear of any bullets that might smash out of the darkness.

No sound – nothing. Frank slowly pulled himself from the wall. He whipped around and through the door, a dark streak of movement, Colt ready to fall and line on flame of gunfire.

He stood within the room, dark and seeming to echo with the sound of his own breathing. He had an instinctive conviction that he was alone. But he did not entirely trust it. Gun ready, he silently groped his way from room to room to the rear. There was no one. He stepped out into the dark yard behind the house and eyed the shadowy shape of the small stable. In a matter of minutes, he learned that it was empty of both men and horses.

He returned to the yard. His eyes narrowed thoughtfully into the darkness. Either Nolan and his hardcases had not yet returned with their prisoners or they had gone somewhere else. Frank realized that in his fear for Dane he had not reasoned clearly.

Nolan was not a fool. He wouldn't stay within reach of marshal and county sheriff – not with Curran murdered. Frank holstered his gun and started around the house toward his waiting horse.

He reached the far corner and heard several riders coming down the street. Frank drew back around the corner, the Colt again in his hand. They were coming back after all! That could mean almost anything. His body felt cold when he thought of Dane.

The horseman came on and drew rein before the house. He heard a low, excited voice when they discovered his horse. Someone answered and Frank started. The voice came again – Ike Jensen's. Frank holstered his gun and stepped clear of the house. Instantly, a voice rapped out a challenge.

'Hold it right there, Mister!'

'Ike! It's me – Frank Barton.'

He strode across the yard. There were half a dozen riders and he made out the sheriff's bulky form as Ike demanded, 'What are you doing here? This is county – not town.'

'I thought I could get Nolan – fast. I forgot boundary lines. But there's no one here.'

'Not even your brother,' another voice asked – Sam Yoder's.

'No.'

Yoder said, 'We saw him with Nolan and those three hardcases in the Geronimo.'

'He was at the Geronimo.' Frank tried to keep the strain from his voice. 'But how do you know he had anything to do with this?'

Jensen cut in, 'The more we jaw, the further away they get. Frank you know the country and I'm going to need you. You're deputized.'

'What!' Yoder blazed. 'Deputize him! He's slow with a gun. He's been playing around with Stevens' daughter. And now his own brother is part of the gang–'

Frank grabbed him by leg and belt and savagely jerked. Yoder came tumbling out of the saddle, swinging wild blows at Frank. They fell in a tangled heap. All of Frank's resentment, fears and uncertainties centred in this man. He wanted to smash him to silence.

He connected a glancing blow at Yoder's face, pale in the darkness. Then clutching hands grabbed Frank. He tried to fight them off, but he was pulled away from Yoder. Jensen stepped before him, blocking Yoder's angry attempts to break free. Frank twisted, but strong hands held him.

'Stop it!' Jensen roared.

The two men finally subsided. Jensen glowered at them in turn. 'Yoder, you have no authority in these parts. I deputize who I please. Maybe all you say is true about Frank. But I know him and his record. I'm holding up any doubts I might have.'

He turned to Frank. 'Yoder's marked out clear what other people might be thinking about you. I figure this is your chance to prove 'em wrong – or right. I need you. Yoder has a right to come along. But I can't have two of my own posse fighting one another. Are you willing to forget this for the time being?'

Frank shrugged off the hands that held him. 'I'll do my job.'

'All right,' Jenson said. 'Now how do you figure this kidnapping?'

Yoder growled sullenly. 'It's clear enough to me. Nolan's working with Bix Terry. Terry knows every day he waits means that much more risk of discovery. He's wanted. So he got tired of waiting for Stevens to move.'

'I can see that,' Ike agreed. 'So they've forced Stevens' hand.'

'Stevens shot Bailey,' Yoder said. 'I think that made Terry and Nolan figure Stevens has nerve enough to make a play for them, one at a time. They'd have no chance against his gun. So Nolan and his hardcases – four against one – went after him. They'll force Stevens to tell 'em where the money's hidden and then kill him.'

'They'll *try* to force him,' Frank cut in.

'He's not a man who'll give up easy.'

'But they'll do it,' Yoder snapped. 'And I'd like to know how your brother got mixed up in this.'

'I don't know that he is – or how deep. But if he is in the middle, it was because of some trick of Nolan's. Dane's not outlaw.'

'We'll see,' Yoder said and Frank swayed toward him. Jensen placed a restraining hand on his chest.

'Calm your feathers, Frank. Point is, we have to catch up with those renegades and get Stevens out of their hands. He's the key to the stolen money. Once we've done that, the truth about your brother will come out. Where do you think they'll take Stevens?'

'Anywhere!' Yoder exclaimed. 'You got the whole dam' desert and all the mountains to search.'

Frank said, 'I'd guess they'd take him to Jed's place first. It's isolated and there's a chance the loot is there.'

'Not a chance! Yoder snorted. 'It would've been found by now.'

'Maybe – but Bailey went there. Stevens rode out shortly after he came back. I'd say it's worth a chance.'

'So would I,' Jensen said decisively.

The small posse headed out into the

desert, riding fast. Frank rode beside Jensen, glad that Yoder remained a short distance behind among the other riders. Jensen set a fast pace and the dark miles flowed behind them.

Frank could only think of Dane. A kidnapping and a murder, and the kid in the middle of it! He tried not to believe it, yet there was Peg's statement that the boy had held the horses while the hardcases went inside for Stevens. And Curran had been knifed within twenty feet of where Dane had stood.

Frank felt a sickening, crawling sensation in his stomach. Had bad blood finally controlled the boy, the very thing he had feared all these years? Hadn't someone once said that what you fear most is bound to happen? Then he remembered what Peg had said, that Dane had good, strong qualities, too.

He closed his eyes as they pounded along and mentally prayed that was true. He had to believe it until the very last minute. The thought sustained him until he saw the low, evil shadow of the trees and the ranch house ahead.

Jensen signalled them to a halt. They peered ahead and then Jensen said softly, 'All right, this is the way we'll hit 'em.'

XVII

'Frank, you and Ranson make a wide loop to the back and then drift in. We'll give you ten minutes. Then the rest of us will ride in from the front. If they break out the back, you'll have 'em.'

Frank neck-reined his horse and one of the men moved out beside him. They drifted away into the night and made a wide circuit.

Frank spoke low in the darkness. 'We can move in, now. When we get in closer, we'll leave the horses. We'll make less noise on foot.'

Ranson angled away from him. Together, they'd make too good a target, even in the night. Frank waited a moment and then flicked his reins, moving slowly toward the dark buildings. He saw the shadow of a low stable and some outhouses with satisfaction. They would be cover enough. They'd leave the horses there and cross the yard afoot.

The stable, low and askew, loomed closer. Between it and the next building, Frank caught a move of shadows. He instantly drew rein, eyes probing. He heard a faint creak of saddle leather as a rider from the house approached him. The shadow took more definite shape. One man came directly toward him and discovery was certain. Frank pulled his gun from the holster. He rapped a sharp challenge. At the same time he pulled the hammer, held it posed to drop.

His answer came – a flame of orange and blue spitting toward him. He heard the roar of the Colt and the 'snnkk!' of the bullet through the air. Frank dropped the hammer and his gun bucked against his hand.

He saw a tumbling, dark shape, heard Ranson's yell off to his left. Beyond the house, he heard shouts that must be Jensen and the rest of the posse. They'd be rushing the house now.

Frank spurred his horse. He heard a crashing noise from the front of the house. He could see the rear, the black oblong of the door, the smaller ones of the dark windows. He held his gun ready, expecting an eruption of the remaining outlaws.

There was only silence, muffled sounds from within the house. The door flew open and Frank lifted the Colt. Jensen's voice called out to him. 'Frank?'

'Here!'

'No one inside. What happened out there?'

'I downed one. I'll see if he's dead or alive.'

He turned the horse and rode back. He saw the shape of riderless horse and a shadowy figure sprawled on the ground. Frank swung out of saddle and, gun in hand, moved forward. The horse snorted, tossed its head as Frank came up. His hands touched the saddle, then bulging bags.

A thrill shot through Frank. The stolen money! His free hand swiftly fumbled at the straps as he held his gun and eyes on the prone shape lying a few feet away. The man did not move. Frank's hand plunged inside the saddlebag. His fingers struck a greasy slab of bacon, some cans. Food – not money.

Frank took a step toward the fallen man as he heard Jensen and the others come up behind him. He bent to the man, gun levelled. First his fingers found the gun belt, moved to the holster – empty. In falling, the man had lost his gun. Jensen and the posse circled about Frank as he holstered his gun and struck a match.

The man lay face up. Frank saw the pinched, unshaven features of Blaine, one of the hardcases who had been with Nolan at the Geronimo. He saw the stain on the man's shirt and he ripped away the cloth. The bullet had struck just below the collarbone on the right side, the force of it driving the man from the saddle.

As Frank's fingers probed, Blaine moved his head from side to side and moaned. Frank, working with grim efficiency, untied the kerchief from around Blaine's neck and made a crude compress of it over the wound. By then the man had opened his eyes.

'Will he live?' Jensen asked.

'If we get him to town and a doctor.'

Blaine cursed and gritted his teeth. He tried to sit up and Frank helped him. He swayed then looked slowly about at the shadowy figures looking over him. Frank hunkered back on his heels.

'Where are they?' he asked.

'Go find 'em,' Blaine answered through set teeth.

'You know where they are. How come Nolan left you?'

'Damn' him – and you! You can go to hell.'

'I'd say you'll beat us there.' Frank could not check the question that burst to his lips. 'The kid? What about him?'

'Him!' Blaine said with weak contempt.

'No good. He dragged his spurs from the beginning. I told Nolan...' He lapsed into sick silence.

'What about the boy?' Frank insisted.

'Got yellow when we came out with Stevens. Would've run if Cass hadn't laid a gun barrel over his ear. Couldn't leave him, so...'

Blaine's voice drifted off. Frank could not suppress the deep sigh of relief. He looked up at Jensen and Yoder. The Pinkerton man hunkered down beside him, face thrust into the outlaw's.

'Where's Bix Terry?'

Blaine blinked at him. 'Bix? He stopped a Rurale bullet down in Chihuahua two years ago – dead and buried.'

'Dead! Then where does Nolan fit in?'

'We all rode with Bix down there. Bix told Nolan about this business with Stevens and that he planned to get his share when Stevens got out of jail. Bix gone, Nolan figured he might as well come up and get the money.'

'And you were to follow,' Frank finished.

'We got the word.' Blaine swayed, glared up at them. 'You gonna let me just sit here and die?'

'Where'd you take Stevens?' Jensen asked.

'Find him!'

'Your gang came here,' Jensen said heavily.

Blaine grinned evilly despite the pain of his wound. 'Dumb lawman! They never come anywhere near here. After Bailey was shot, we shacked up here until Nolan sent for us. I come to pick up our camp supplies.'

'So now they'll run short of food in the hideout,' Frank cut in. 'Where is it?'

'You find it!'

Blaine suddenly fell over. Jensen cursed under his breath and Frank swiftly examined the renegade. He breathed and Frank looked around as Jensen asked, 'What in hell will we do now? According to him, we can't pick up a trail. They didn't even come here.'

Frank thought of Dane. The kid had undoubtedly still been drunk as he held the horses. Then, when he found out what he was into, he had tried to quit the bunch. Outlaws like Blaine or Nolan didn't let anyone quit. They'd kill first. Grimly, Frank worked over the man until his eyes opened again.

'Where'd they go?' Frank demanded.

No answer. Jensen tried to pry the information from him, and so did Yoder. Twice more, Blaine passed out and finally

Jensen stood up.

'Hell, we're getting nowhere. He needs a doctor.'

'I need my brother,' Frank snapped and slapped Blaine's face. He spoke over his shoulder as he worked. 'I'll get it out of him if I have to kill him.'

'Now, Frank–'

'I mean it, Ike. You've got one murder now. Do you want two more – Dane and Stevens?'

The sheriff grunted and sank back on his heels, watching Frank's grim face and his slapping hands. At long last, the outlaw came around again. Frank let Blaine lie sprawled until he again tried to sit up. Once more Frank helped him and the renegade growled weakly.

'I'm losing blood. You gonna let me die?'

'Maybe – one way or another.'

'You can't. I got a right to a doctor.'

Frank cursed him and then said more quietly, 'So you've got rights? You expect us to take you to town, get you patched up. Then you figure on a cell and a trial that you hope you can beat. Well, forget it.'

'I know the law!'

'I bet you do – you've broken enough of them.' Frank's fingers taloned into Blaine's cheeks on either side of his mouth. He jerked Blaine's head up so that he could look into the dark shadows of the eyes.

'That kid Nolan has is my brother. Understand that! If he's not dead now, he will be as soon as Nolan figures he doesn't need him or the kid's in the way. Do you think I'll stop at anything to find him?'

'Then find him!' Blaine made weak defiance.

Frank drew his Colt and pressed the cold muzzle against the outlaw's head. Blaine tried to jerk away but Frank's fingers, clawed into his cheeks, held his head.

'You won't do it!' Blaine babbled. 'You're a lawman and–'

'Won't I!'

The hammer dogged back and the click sounded loud and ominous in the suddenly stilled circle of men. The outlaw's eyes rolled toward the gun.

'Frank,' Jensen protested, 'I won't let you–'

'Ike, don't make a move. I'll let the hammer drop, so help me!' He never took his eyes from Blaine and now his voice sank low, almost to a whisper.

'I said you'd be in hell before us and you're standing on the edge of it right now.

206

A forty-four slug will push you over unless you start talking in the next five seconds.'

His voice dropped to a deadly note. 'One ... two ... three...'

XVIII

'...Four...'

'Wait! Wait now.'

Frank still held the gun at Blaine's head. The outlaw cast his eyes at the others and then capitulated. 'Up in the hills beyond here. There's an old homestead shack Cass found while he nosed around, waiting for Stevens to get out of jail. Just what we wanted.'

'Where would that be?' Frank growled.

'Go to the place where Bailey was shot. Canyon just beyond it leads up in the hills. Opens onto a valley. On the far side, there's another canyon. Through it and you'll come on the shack.'

'I think there's a big rock chimney close by,' Frank said slowly.

'That's the one. Now I've told you. Ease down that hammer.'

Frank lowered the Colt but did not holster it. 'Does Nolan intend to camp out there, figuring things will blow over?'

'Just long enough to find where that

money's hidden. He'll torture it out of Stevens if he has to.'

'He might.' Frank holstered the gun and turned to Jensen. 'That's all we need. Let's ride.'

'Wait, Frank. Nolan's holed up with two gunslingers. It could take some doing to force our way through if that canyon's any kind of a fort. We'd better get some more men – and we can't let this skunk die out here even if he oughta.'

Frank made an impatient sound but he knew Ike made sense. He choked back irritation nodded, then swung on the outlaw again. 'Who killed Curran?'

'Not me, Mister. You can't hang me for that!'

'Who, then?'

'Nolan. The kid had just tried to make his break and Nolan knocked him out. Then we saw this gent back in the shadows and we threw guns on him. Nolan said he was a railroad dick and we couldn't take him along.'

'So you knifed him,' Frank's voice shook, 'in cold blood.'

'Nolan did. I don't even own a knife. Never did. Nolan knocked him out and then used the knife – quieter.'

Jensen said in a sick voice, 'Get him on a horse, someone.'

Frank rode back to Apache Crossing with the posse, so relived that Dane was cleared that he almost felt light headed. Dane, as Peg had said, had drawn back from crime. Thank God for that!

They came into the town and rode directly to the Geronimo. Jensen told Frank to jail the prisoner and call the doctor. He pulled his gun from the holster and fired it into the air three times.

'Do you know any quicker way to call up the town?' he answered their puzzled stares.

As Frank crossed the street to the jail, leading the horse on whose back the outlaw clung, he saw men erupt from the saloons. He helped the renegade down and half dragged him to a cell. When he came out and hurried away for the doctor he saw men milling about Ike as more hurried down the street.

A murder, Frank thought grimly, a kid-napping, chance of two more murders. That was enough in itself to cause men to help the law. But add the chance of actually finding the stolen money and Ike would have no trouble gathering a posse.

He took the doctor to the jail. Ike still

gathered townsmen before the Geronimo and now he sent them scurrying for weapons and food. It would be a little while before they rode out. Frank hurried to the hotel.

He ran up the steps to the porch and Peg materialized from the shadows, throwing herself in his arms. She held him a second and then straightened. 'Tell me! Dane? Jed? You found them? They're all right?'

He told her what had happened, that the posse intended to track Nolan down. He did not add the grim thought there was a chance Dane and Jed would be dead before they cornered Nolan.

'Cass Nolan!' he ended. 'Bix Terry's outlaw friend came in here months before Stevens was due out of prison. Rents a place and makes himself part of the town. No one knew him – not even Jed. Peg, he fooled us all.'

'Can Jed really tell him where the money is?'

He knew what she meant – had her stepfather been guilty all along? He nodded slowly. 'Nolan knew exactly what happened from Bix Terry. He did not go to all this trouble and risk if he wasn't sure. He *knew*, Peg. That's more than any of us did – except Stevens.'

211

The light from the lobby streamed out, revealing her face. Her lips painfully moved and her eyes closed as her fingers tightened on Frank's arms and then eased off. 'Frank, I – think I knew, too. I just hoped differently, and too much.'

A lift of voices from the gathering posse came to them. He swiftly kissed her. 'I have to go.'

'Frank, if you find Dane and – he is well – bring him here. Please?'

Frank nodded and hurried to the street. He went into his office, emptied shell boxes into his pockets and then went out to his horse at the rack. He swung into saddle and rode across the street, working his way through mounted men to Ike's side.

'You ready?' Ike asked.

'More than ready.'

'We'll ride then.' He looked up to the night sky. 'No moon, few stars. It'll be damned near pitch dark.'

'Enough to see most of the way, at least deep into the mountains.'

'Frank, I head this posse.' Frank looked at him in surprise and the sheriff went on. 'I know what's driving you – your brother. It's driving me, too. But not hard enough I'd lose my way in a maze of canyons because I couldn't wait until daylight. Understand?'

'Sure, but I know that country.'

'And I know when it gets too dark to pick up a trail or find one canyon in a hundred. I'll call camp if we need to.'

He reined his horse about and his heavy voice lifted in a shout that called the attention of the milling, waiting riders. His arm, signal waved them out and they cantered down the street, a cloud of dust kicking up behind them, to be instantly lost in the night and the shadows.

It was but a few hours to dawn when Ike called a halt deep in the broken, mountain country. Frank made an impatient sound but the sheriff disregarded him, speaking to the others.

'It's not long before light, so we'll wait until we can see our hands before our noses. Rest your horses and your muscles. Get some sleep if you can. Come dawn, we'll look on a hard day.'

There was no dissent except Frank's. He reluctantly dismounted and stamped his feet to relieve cramped muscles. Men moved here and there, some aimlessly. A match flared and small flames licked greedily, grew larger. Frank moved toward the fire. He grudgingly admitted Ike had been wise. He could not tell one peak from another.

'*Senor* Marshal!'

He looked up, surprised, into Manuel's broad, wide smile. 'I didn't know you'd come along.'

'*Si!* It is your brother up there, eh? – and *Senor* Stevens?'

'Sure, but–'

Manuel's smiled vanished. 'I always think you are my friend. That is so, eh?'

'Of course, Manuel–'

'Then when my friend need help, he get help. Same way *Senor* Stevens up there. He once try to help with Ernesto and he good friend even if he go to prison. So?'

'So thanks, Manuel.'

The big man's grin flashed again. 'Hah! that is better. He sobered. '*Senor*, the boy. He will be all right. I know it.'

'Let's hope.'

Frank moved away. Men sat about the fire. They talked eagerly to one another. Some yawned and tried to snatch a bit of sleep before dawn. Frank could neither sleep nor rest. He moved beyond the group, out toward the dark, close pressing mountains. The darkness hid him from the rest.

Dane filled his mind and he wanted to forge ahead into the night. But Sheriff

Jensen was right. Frank told himself it was just a short time to dawn and he tried to turn his thoughts elsewhere.

Manuel Perez – the Mexican's heart was as big as his body. And how pathetic his gratitude for what little Stevens had been able to do for his brother! Still, it was enough for Manuel – and so he rode tonight.

Frank's mind fastened on this in order to exclude Dane. He strolled more slowly now in a wide half circle about the distant fire and the men. He recalled Stevens' wry comment about the covering on the well.

'My sole monument and I bet it's getting rotten.'

What a hell of a way to summarize a life! Frank wondered what made Stevens go wrong when he had made a reputation for himself as a lawman. Money, of course, first the petty blackmail and then the train and the big haul. But those things were only an ending, indicating a basic weakness in the man's character.

Frank turned sharply toward the fire. Why try to answer that question? If they had any luck tomorrow and Stevens was rescued along with Dane, Frank would ask him. At least for tonight and the moment, these thoughts had checked Frank's fear for Dane and his foolish impatience. He found a bare spot near the fire and settled down.

Time passed tortuously. Frank set himself for patience and would find himself intently watching the dark eastern sky. He'd try to forget it. If he did, he thought of Dane and the cold worry would come that the boy might already be dead. He'd shove that out of his mind with thought of Stevens. Maybe Nolan had already worked the secret of the hidden money from him. In that case, Nolan would kill his captives, grab the loot and disappear. That would bring Frank right back to Dane again. So the night wore on.

At last there was gray in the east, strengthening as the possemen rose, stretched, nursed cramp muscles, cursed. A breeze sprang up as red tinged the dawning blue above the barren peaks. Frank was first in the saddle. Jensen rode up, eyes red with need for rest.

'Are we close to the canyon?'

Frank gestured northward. 'Maybe ten miles. When we come out of this draw, we ought to see that rock chimney.'

'Well, that's something. You know the way. Lead out.'

They threaded the canyon, Frank in

advance. As he predicted, the canyon opened into a long, wide valley, bounded on the far side by another backbone of peaks in this complex of mountains. Frank's eyes swung westward as Ike came up and he pointed.

Across the valley and some distance to the left, stood the crooked, angular spire of the rock chimney formed by centuries' erosion of wind and sand. Frank led the posse into the desert valley.

Half way out, he drew rein and pointed ahead and to the ground. Jensen looked and his head swivelled back to Frank. 'Tracks. Fresh.'

The rest of the posse moved up. One of them, looked more closely at the tracks, eyes following the run of them. 'Five riders, I'd say.'

'Nolan,' Frank counted, 'two hardcases, Dane and Stevens. They're alive then – at least, last night.'

Jensen nodded and signalled the posse to follow as he rode along the new trail. It cut diagonally across the valley toward the mountains. The rock chimney loomed higher and then sank below the peaks as the riders approached the base of the mountains.

A canyon opened out before them. Jensen

reined in. 'Is this it, Frank?'

'Has to be, from what the renegade said.'

He impatiently lifted the reins but Ike checked him. 'I know how you feel. But don't rush in blind and don't try to leave us behind. You might need every one of our guns.'

Frank grunted and touched the horse into motion, heading into the canyon. At first it was wide, the rock walls not very high. Frank's narrowed eyes cast along the crest to either side, spotting every likely spot where a rifleman could hide.

The canyon walls pinched in as it made erratic turns deeper into the mountains. The rims lifted steadily as the canyon narrowed. Heat increased as the sun rose higher. Frank rounded a turn. For a short distance, the canyon led straight ahead to where the frowning walls pinched in even more so that barely one man could ride along. Frank halted and Jensen and the riders crowded up close behind him.

'Close?' the sheriff asked.

'A mile or two, from what Blaine said.'

'End of trail,' Jensen said and waved them on.

Frank moved out ahead. He saw a puff of smoke high on one of the narrow walls. The rifle slug gouted sand beneath his horse and Frank savagely reined in, his hand snaking his Colt from the holster. The hidden rifle cracked again and the slug missed, fanning by Frank's body.

'Back up!' Jensen ordered behind Frank.

A voice came to them, flattened by distance and the bouncing echo of the walls but recognizable – Nolan's.

'Barton!'

Frank stiffened, looked upward toward the voice, saw nothing but the walls. The voice came again. 'Barton, are you smart?'

Frank cupped his hands around his mouth and yelled, 'What do you want, Nolan?'

'Not a damn' thing you can give me. But you want something – your brother.'

'How about Stevens?'

'To hell with him – now. I've got Dane. Tell you something else. This canyon's the only way you can get through. I hold aces.'

'Wait'll you get hungry.'

Nolan ignored the thrust. 'Call off the posse, Barton. Don't try to rush us. If you do, Dane will be the first to die.'

XIX

Frank stiffened and Ike grabbed his arm. Frank moved to throw it off. 'Frank, don't try it. Nolan would be just the killer to do what he says.'

Frank's shoulders slumped. He turned his horse and slowly rode back around the bend with Ike to join the posse. Jensen dryly outlined the situation.

'It's a stand-off. We can't get by that hole in the wall without some of us drawing bullets.'

Frank blazed, 'He could kill Dane and Stevens and be half way across Arizona by nightfall.'

'He can't,' Ike said grimly. 'We're too close for him to try to run. So he'll sit tight until he figures it out.'

'And so will we,' Frank said, 'giving him plenty of time to work over Stevens and kill Dane when he's ready.'

'What can we do? That sidewinder won't make terms.'

Frank looked back toward the narrow pass. 'I want a chance to get Dane out, maybe Stevens.'

'How?' Yoder asked harshly. 'We can't get in. Do we risk a bullet because your brother–'

'You risk nothing! I do.' Frank turned to Jensen. 'There must be other ways into that hideout. I want a chance to find one. If Nolan's watching and sees a bunch of us ride off, he'll figure we're trying to circle in or cut him off. He'll act fast. But he won't miss one man.'

'Makes sense,' Ike said slowly.

'It's all we can do. Plug him up here and keep his attention. Give me until morning, anyhow.'

'What would you do if you did get to Nolan?' Yoder asked sceptically. 'So far as we know he's as fast as Stevens and sure as hell faster than Bailey. He'd gun you down.'

Frank flushed but ignored the thrust. He looked appealingly at Jensen. 'I should at least have a chance to get Dane.'

Manuel Perez called, '*Senor* Sheriff, I go with him. Two guns better than one, no?'

The sheriff looked sharply from Manuel to Frank, then peered down the canyon. 'You got your chance, Frank. We'll pin Nolan down here.'

Frank lifted the reins and rode back through the posse, Manuel falling in beside

221

him as they retraced their way down the canyon. The other riders watched after them until Ike broke the silence.

Frank and Manuel rode down the canyon to the place where it opened into the wide valley. Frank tried to thank Manuel, but the man waved it aside. They came out into the valley and the rock chimney's spire loomed against the sky, yellow now in the hot rays of the sun. Frank thumbed back his hat and looked westward along the line of mountains. No other canyons threaded them and Manuel's dark face fell when he, too, realized they faced a rock barrier.

'What we do?'

Frank turned his horse westward and spoke grimly over his shoulder. 'Hope to God we find a way in!'

For several miles the high face of the peaks offered a solid barrier. Frank clamped down on the beginnings of despair and rode on. A mile or so beyond, the escarpment was broken by a narrow passage, hardly wide enough for one rider. It might pinch in and close within a matter of yards, Frank knew, but he turned into it.

High, close walls made him feel as though he entered a tunnel and the sound of the horse, the creak of leather was loud. Ahead, the passage made a turn and Frank literally held his breath until they rounded it and he saw the canyon continue to another turn not far ahead.

So it went, turn after turn, as they penetrated deeper into the mountains. The two men rode silently and grimly, success alternating with fear of failure, to lift to hope again.

Frank rounded a corner and he saw, some distance ahead, that the canyon opened on a small barren mountain valley. In a few moments, they rode out into it. At first glance, Frank thought they had come into a cul-de-sac and his heart plummeted.

But Manuel pointed to the right. 'Over there.'

Frank saw the narrow opening. This new canyon was as narrow as the needle they had threaded behind them. But soon the walls fell back and finally Manuel could come up beside Frank. Their hopes rose. The sun was now directly overhead and the canyon became an oven. But they plodded on.

The canyon led them in the general direction of the hideout. Then it made a turn westward, in the wrong direction. But they could only continue along it. At least, it led deeper into the heart of the mountains.

Frank had not realized the extent of this broken country, the number of canyons that threaded it like crooked snakes, the small heat blasted pockets upon which the canyons opened. There were heartbreaking detours during which he and Manuel despaired of winning through. And then another canyon would take them in the direction they wanted to go.

Late afternoon they came out into another of those pockets, wider than the rest. As Frank rode into it, he suddenly straightened and drew rein.

'Manuel! There!'

The big Mexican followed the direction of his pointing finger. Beyond and above the rock escarpment, he saw the crooked spire of the stone chimney. His sweaty face broke into a broad smile.

'We are close, *Senor!*'

Frank spoke slowly. 'I figure that rock ridge is between us and the posse in the canyon. Then Nolan's hideout must be ... in that direction.'

Manuel's face fell. 'But the ridge, *Senor*. Over there, it turns back toward us.'

'I know.' Frank lifted the reins. 'But luck's been with us, so maybe that ridge breaks the other way and we'll find a way through or over it.'

He touched the horse into motion, cutting across the pocket and Manuel followed, muttering prayers to the saints. Again they threaded canyons and the rock escarpment always offered a final, tantalizing barrier to them. The sun moved westward and Frank felt the pressure of time. They needed daylight to thread these rocks.

The sky slowly darkened, purple shadows formed and still there seemed to be no way to their goal. Frank pressed grimly on, throwing an angry look at the sky above the peaks.

A few moments later, they came to another narrow crevice that led into the rock barrier. Frank turned into it with no real hope, Manuel following. It made many twists and turns and, down in here, the shadows of coming night lurked about them.

They took another turn and Frank's eyes widened. They had come through! Ahead was the mouth of the canyon. In a few moments they came out into a wide valley. Frank saw a low, scabrous house and a spidery corral. To the south, he saw rock peaks hemming in that side of the valley, the black gash that marked a canyon. It had to be the one that the posse bottled up.

'*Senor*,' Manuel said softly, 'Over there.'

He pointed. Three horses grazed behind the house. Frank could not tell at this distance whether they were on picket, but they were not saddled. He made count. Nolan, two gunslingers, Dane and Stevens – five men, three horses, so men still guarded the canyon.

A light glowed from one of the windows of the house. Frank looked to the sky, purpling but shot with golden and fiery red streaks of the sun somewhere behind the peaks.

'We'll wait until full dark,' he said. 'No use taking a chance someone will see us trying to get to the house. We're this close and we know they're not gone.'

They moved back into the canyon and dismounted. Despite impatience, it was good to walk about in small circles, stretching aching muscles. They checked their guns and set themselves to wait, watching the house.

Night came on. A few stars showed and then the buildings and corrals faded into the black shadows that filled the valley. Frank stood up.

'We drift in.'

They mounted and moved slowly toward

the steady glow of light that marked a window. Frank probed the darkness for a lookout, glanced toward the distant canyon mouth. Nothing moved, there was no alarm. Slowly, as they approached, the silhouette of the buildings took shape out of the dark. Frank reined in.

'They'll hear the horses if we ride closer,' he said. 'You circle to the far side, dismount and move.'

'You, *Senor?*'

'I'm drifting in right now. You keep out of sight but back any play I make. If you see I'm in trouble, come helling.'

Manuel nodded and in another moment was lost in the night. Frank dismounted, ground-tied the horse. He moved in slowly toward the house, lining on the lighted window. Now and then he stopped to listen. Then he'd move on.

He came close to the house, moved to one side to avoid the lamp light streaming from the uncurtained window. Slowly he drifted in and finally pressed against the wall, still warm from the day's sun.

He heard a voice and recognized Nolan's. 'I'm running low on patience, Stevens. Maybe you figure I can't do more'n what I have. Well, change your mind.'

'Go to hell.' Stevens' even voice came to Frank.

Frank edged to the window. Slowly, carefully, he looked within the room. It was filthy, dusty, sparsely furnished. Frank saw Nolan's broad back as the man stood spread legged, beefy hands on hips above the heavy cartridge belt. Then Frank saw the bunk in the far corner. Dane lay upon it, ankles and arms tied.

The boy had a welt along his cheek where he had taken a blow. His clothing and hair was disarrayed, his dark face flushed. But there was more anger than fear in his eyes and Frank felt a surge of pride in his brother.

Nolan moved and Frank saw Stevens. He was lashed to a chair, boots and socks pulled off. There was no sign of the gunhawks, so they must be up in the canyon holding down the posse.

Nolan went to a rickety table, returned with a sliver of wood in his hand. He glared at Stevens. 'Once more, where did you hide the money?'

'You're wasting your breath.'

'And you're asking for a slug.'

'You won't kill me. You'd lose the whole gamble if you did. I won't do you any good dead.'

Nolan pulled a heavy knife from his pockets, snapped open the long, sharp blade and worked on the sliver of wood. 'Bix Terry told me the whole set-up. He and his partner robbed the train. They passed the money to Bailey while you bought drinks at the Cattleman, setting up an alibi. You slipped out and met Rance, who gave you the money while he went into the Geronimo. You hid it.'

'Bix always could spin a story,' Stevens said.

Nolan snapped the blade shut. 'He had no reason to lie to his best friend when he was dying. I give you credit for working out a neat job. If Bix's partner hadn't been shot and talked, it'd been perfect.'

Nolan grinned cruelly down at Stevens. 'Except there'd have been four ways to divide it, wouldn't there? The partner's dead – so's Bix. You killed Bailey. That just leaves you. Now, through lying? Are you going to tell me where it is?'

'Go ahead,' Stevens said flatly. 'Kill me.'

'Oh, no! I'm not losing the money after riding all that distance and taking these risks. I intend to find out what you know.'

He gabbed one of Stevens' bare feet. Viciously, he jabbed the sharpened splinter under a toenail. Stevens could not suppress a cry of pain and then he bit down on his lip and was silent. Nolan studied him.

'Talking?'

Stevens endured the pain. Nolan went to the table. He came back with another splinter. He watched Stevens' pale, sweating face as he sharpened it.

Frank clenched his teeth, his lips peeled back. He checked an impulse to break in. He looked toward the front corner of the house, back at the widow. Nolan moved, catching Frank's attention. Dane, over on the bunk, looked pale and sick.

'One more, my friend?' Nolan asked softly. 'Or do you talk?'

Frank held himself unmoving, praying Stevens would talk. If he did, he'd disclose the money cache. If he didn't, Frank knew he could no longer stand by. Out of danger, Stevens would never talk and all of them, would be right back at the beginning so far as the loot was concerned.

Nolan held up the sharpened splinter, heavy face alight in a smile of sheer enjoyment. He bent down to Stevens' foot and the man tried to twist free. Nolan held it, place the splinter against the toe preparatory to driving it home beneath the nail.

'This time, I'll put a match to it.'

Stevens suddenly collapsed. 'You win. You'll kill me, but it's better than this.'

All Frank's attention centred on the room inside. Nolan didn't move but held the splinter poised.

'Well, now! Talk.'

Stevens hesitated and Nolan exerted pressure on the wooden sliver. Stevens winced, jerked. 'Wait! I'll tell you. I'll lead you to it.'

'Where?'

'In town. That's where it's been all along.'

Frank didn't hear any sound behind him. But suddenly the hard round muzzle of a gun pressed against his back. He jerked, froze. A harsh voice called behind him.

'Cass! We got us a visitor!'

XX

Frank's gun lifted from his holster and the rough voice growled, 'Around to the front. I'm hoping you try to make a break.'

Frank turned slowly and walked carefully, the man with the gun a step or two behind. He turned the corner, stepped up on the porch as Nolan threw open the door. Frank entered, his captor behind him.

'Frank!' Dane exclaimed from the bunk. He tried to get up but fell back.

Nolan's blue eyes held a pleased light as he looked at Frank. He threw a question at the renegade, one of those Frank had seen in town. The man told where he had caught Frank.

'How about the posse?'

'Not a sound out of them, Cass. They pulled back around that turn and there they've stayed. Show themselves now and then and that's all.'

Nolan smiled tightly at Frank. 'A cute little trick, Marshal. Your friends keep us watching them while you come in from another direction. I warned you what would happen to Dane.'

Frank spoke quickly, 'Wait, Nolan. I slipped away from the posse. Found my way up here. You hold aces, so – I'll trade myself for the kid. It still gives you a hostage.'

Nolan considered him and then slowly smiled. 'For a minute I nearly believed you.' His eyes jumped beyond Frank to the renegade. 'Get Cross – fast. We're pulling out. Our friend'll take us to the money.'

'Where?'

'In town.'

'In town! Cass, that's putting our necks in a noose.'

Nolan chuckled. 'It'll take the posse a long time to learn we've pulled out. The Marshal here will take us out the way he come in. If he don't...' Nolan's glance at Dane completed the threat. 'We'll ride to town, get the money and be gone before that posse's found its way back out of the mountains.'

Dane again tried to free himself but subsided when Frank gave him a small, quick signal. Nolan, moving to one side, waved Frank over with a motion of his gun. He spoke to the renegade.

'Meader, put our friend's boots back on while I watch the marshal. Then ride out for

Cross. Get back here quick.'

The outlaw bent to the task and Jed bit back an exclamation of pain when the man pulled the boot over his tortured toe. Then Meader, with a sharp look at Nolan, went out, closing the door behind him.

Nolan looked around the room. 'I sure picked up a fine collection. There's you, Marshal, fool enough to come bumbling in. There's Dane, a kid I thought might work into a good sidekick. But he didn't have the chips when the showdown came. So I figured he'd make a good hostage – and he has.'

Nolan's glance cut to Stevens and his smile widened. 'And Jed Stevens, who knows where all that nice money's hidden. A heap of people looking for it – including you, Marshal – but it's going where it'll do the most good. Right in my own pocket.'

He chuckled and took a step to the center of the room. 'Now we'll all rest comfortable until Meader and Cross get back.'

Frank backed into a corner on Nolan's sharp order. Dane quietly but uselessly strained at his bonds. Stevens sagged against the rope that held him to the chair. His eyes were closed, fighting pain and despair.

Frank wondered where Manuel could be.

He listened for faint sound but none came. Nolan, seated in a chair in a far corner where he could watch all of them, held his gun in his lap. But it could snap up, line and fire before Frank could jump across the room.

Dragging minutes passed. Frank could only wait them out. Stevens finally lifted his head, his flecked eyes clear again. He studied Nolan, then Frank and his lips faintly thinned beneath the mustache. Nolan moved restlessly. He stood up and started to pace. Frank watched him, muscles tense, but Nolan kept at a safe distance. He came in line with a window.

A gun blasted. The glass smashed into a thousand pieces and the slug whined across the room, thudded into the far wall. Nolan crouched, wheeled about to the window, gun lining on it.

Frank propelled himself across the room. Nolan realized his mistake, started to whirl around. Frank reached him, swung for his jaw as he grabbed for the gun. His blow staggered Nolan and Frank's fingers clamped around the man's gun wrist.

Nolan tried to whip free but Frank hung on, slamming his fist into the broad face. Nolan grunted and blood gushed from his nose. He brought up his fist in a slamming blow at Frank's stomach. Frank twisted so that the knuckles grazed across his ribs. But the blow still had force enough to make him gasp.

As he whirled around with Nolan, fighting to get the gun, he glimpsed Stevens tugging against his bonds, his chair tipping over to the floor. Dane struggled wildly on the bunk.

Frank and Nolan whirled across the room, slammed into the wall and fell to the floor beside Dane's bunk in a thrashing, fighting tangle of arms and legs. The door crashed open and Manuel jumped in, gun held poised.

Nolan managed to come to his knees, Frank pinned beneath him but grimly holding on to his gun wrist. Nolan glared, lifted his fist to slam it into Frank's face. Dane drew up his bound legs and lashed straight out with all the power of his body.

His boot heels struck Nolan in the back of the head. The big man catapulted over Frank, muscles going slack. He smashed into the floor.

Frank whipped about and scrambled for the gun that had gone skittering toward Stevens, who now struggled against the ropes and the chair on the floor. Frank scooped up the gun and whipped around. Nolan lay still, knocked out.

A gun roared from outside, the bullet whipping through the open door. Manuel made a choked sound and fell forward, his weapon flying toward Nolan from his slack fingers.

Frank swung his gun at the lamp. The heavy barrel broke the chimney, snuffed out the flame. He twisted about and fired through the open door into the darkness.

Dane yelled desperately, 'Frank! Get me loose!'

Another bullet whipped into the room, a wild shot, fired blindly. Frank saw the tongue of bright flame far out in the yard and he slammed a shot toward it. He whipped about then and jumped to the bunk.

His groping fingers found a knot, tugged at it. He felt it loosen but just then another probing shot slammed into the room. Frank jumped to the door, leaving Dane to finish freeing himself. He saw a flitting shadow out in the yard, fired. Someone cursed.

He heard hoof beats, racing horses, and the sound swiftly diminished. Meader had returned with Cross, Frank knew, and had caught Manuel framed in the doorway. They had taken a hand but Frank's return fire had been too much.

He listened to the fading sound. The renegades had sensed disaster and had abandoned Nolan, thinking only to save themselves.

Dane's voice lifted in a straining yell. 'Frank! Watch out! Nolan–'

Frank dropped into a crouch. A long flame of red and orange licked toward him out of the darkness. Frank's Colt lifted and roared in its turn as he placed the slug just above the lance of flame. There was a heavy crash and then silence except for the fading thunder of the guns in the small room.

Frank waited. Dane's choked voice came from out of the darkness. 'He's down, Frank. Wait a minute. I'm almost free. I'll see.'

'Careful!' Frank snapped.

He heard movements and then Dane's relieved sigh. 'He's not moving. I'll strike a match.'

The small flame flared and Frank saw Nolan sprawled on a floor in the corner where the slug had driven him. The small light went out but Frank had seen the dark stain on the man's chest.

He stood up, holstering his gun, as Dane struck another match, going into the next room. He returned with a lighted lamp and a single look at Nolan told Frank that the man was dead. He turned to Manuel, felt a clutch of fear as he saw the dark red shine of blood on the man's scalp.

He rolled Manuel over. The man's eyes opened and he looked hazily at Frank, who expelled his breath in 'whoosh!' of relief. For a moment Manuel looked blankly at him and then he jerked up to a sitting position, grabbed his head in pain.

'*Madre de Dios!*'

Frank's quick examination of the wound showed it to be a deep scalp cut. The big man had missed death by a whisper. Frank stood up, turned as Dane untied Stevens. The boy looked up at his brother as he worked.

'Frank.'

'Yes?'

The boy indicated Nolan's body. 'I reckon I still need a big brother. I caused a lot of trouble.'

'It's all right, Dane. I had something to learn, too.' He caught the new light in Dane's face. Frank added gruffly, 'We can't hole up here all night.'

Not long afterward, Frank led the procession down the narrow way of the canyon.

It was pitch dark and they had to ride slowly. Dane rode behind Frank, after him came Stevens, crippled by torture but still shrewd and dangerous, Frank knew. So Manuel rode behind Stevens, leading a horse across which Nolan's heavy body was tied.

They came to the narrow neck of the canyon and Frank shouted ahead for Jensen. There was an answering halloo, filled with sharp suspicion. Frank identified himself and was ordered forward.

'Slow and easy,' Jensen's heavy voice warned, 'until we can take a look at you.'

The posse was stunned to see them. Yoder most of all. He looked at Nolan's body, then Stevens and back to Frank. He said grudgingly, 'Well, looks like a clean-up. I guess I was wrong about you.'

Frank turned away but Yoder spoke sharply. 'So Stevens talked. Where's the money?'

'In town.'

'In town! Where?'

'Nolan didn't get that far,' Frank said shortly. 'Ask Stevens.'

Jensen checked Yoder as he started toward Stevens. 'He can wait, Sam. We're riding out now. When we get to town–'

'You're wasting your breath,' Stevens said wearily. 'I lied to Nolan – playing for time.'

Frank shook his head. 'You're lying now. Nolan had you beat, and talking.'

Well, Marshal,' Stevens' voice held a new and strengthening lift, 'that's something you have to prove.'

Frank turned away and soon the posse started the long ride back through the mountains. As they rode, Frank thought of Stevens' new confidence and knew that, safe from Nolan, he felt his secret was safe. The law could not hold Stevens and the man knew it. So far as Yoder, Grange, Jensen and himself were concerned, they were right back to the moment when Stevens was released from prison.

Not quite. Bailey was dead, and Nolan. In killing Nolan, Frank had redeemed himself from the stigma Bailey had put upon him. More important, Dane had come back, the boy having found new values for himself. This time, Frank vowed, he'd advise Dane, not rule him. The strength of blood and character had come out, not the weakness.

Frank's thoughts returned to Stevens. Back where they started. Not quite back, Frank amended again. They had narrowed the circle, if you could call the whole town of Apache Crossing as a narrowing.

Frank rode silently with the posse. Sometimes his thoughts would dwell on Dane, and Frank knew pride in his younger brother. Again, he could try to think where in the town the money could be hidden. Again, he'd think of those bad, gun filled seconds with Bailey and the strained time that followed, or the swift, deadly action with Nolan. That made him think of Manuel and Frank glanced at the big Mexican with the white bandage wrapped about his skull. That furrowing bullet had nearly sent Manuel to join Ernesto, long dead now.

It was dawn by the time the posse rode wearily into town. Jensen ordered someone to take care of Nolan's body and told Frank to see that Manuel and Stevens went to the doctor so that wounded head and tortured foot could be checked.

Yoder, deep lines of fatigue about his mouth and eyes, dismounted and glared at Stevens. Jed, understanding, grinned back and Yoder huffily stomped off.

Dane went with Frank to the doctor. They left Manuel and Stevens with him and the brothers wearily walked back down the main street. The stores and buildings were silent and aloof in the bright, unreal early morning light. The two men approached the hotel.

Peg hurried out and Frank knew she had spent a sleepless night. She stood poised at the top of the steps and relief flooded her drawn face. Frank bounded up the steps and she came into his arms. He kissed her and saw Dane grinning at them from the foot of the steps.

Peg flushed, recovered. 'You two need something to eat – and rest.'

'Coffee will do, Peg, if you have it.'

She led the way through the silent, sleeping building to the kitchen. They sat down at a table as Peg prepared the coffee. They told her all that had happened.

'And Jed?'

'He'll be along when the doctor's patched up his foot,' Frank answered. 'Peg, he did steal that money. He knows where it is.'

Peg sighed and poured the steaming coffee. 'I think I always knew but wouldn't quite admit it. Last night, I had nothing to do but worry about you and think – about Jed. I realized that he has been tricky, cruel and selfish to everyone but me. I knew that I was the exception, not the rule.'

'Peg, some liked him. Manuel, for instance, even though Ernesto's death was never solved.'

She sat down. 'I suppose he'll get in more

trouble.' Frank didn't answer. He looked startled and thoughtful. He came suddenly to his feet. He caught himself, looked down at Peg, dark eyes sorrowful and questioning.

'Peg, I think I'm going to have to arrest him.'

Her eyes widened. 'Something—'

'I can't tell you. I can't be sure, yet. But it makes sense. I have to, Peg. I'm a lawman.'

Her eyes clouded. 'I understand. If it's a crime... I know what he is now. I know what you are ... and I love you. Nothing changes that.'

He leaned toward her, face softening. The he abruptly straightened. 'I depend on that. Dane, come with me.'

He hurried to the doctor's office, glancing toward the livery stable as he crossed the street. Jensen and some of the posse were still there. Frank hurried on. As he approached the doctor's office, Jed and Manuel came out.

Frank ordered, 'Stevens, come with me.'

'Now why is that, Marshal? I need some rest.'

'You'll get it, after we talk to the sheriff.'

'Is this an arrest?'

'Not yet. Depends. Are you coming?'

Stevens moistened his lips and his right

244

hand slowly moved up and down his right leg as though regretting the absence of holster and gun. He shrugged and came on down the steps.

Ike Jensen and the few remaining posse members, among them Sam Yoder, looked around in surprise as Frank and his brother, with Stevens and Manuel, came up.

'Something wrong?' Jensen asked.

'No, something's right. I know where that stolen money's hidden.'

Stevens finally broke the stunned silence. 'You're a liar!'

'We'll see. Ike, get some shovels and a crowbar.'

Stevens' eyes mirrored a sudden uneasiness. Jensen spoke to one of the posse. 'I know the livery stable will have shovels. Might have a crowbar. Go see.'

In a few moments, Frank led the procession across the street, between two buildings and down the alley toward Manuel's *cantina*. He stopped before the old well.

'Uncover it.'

The men went to work with the crowbar and ancient nails complained as they were pulled loose. Jensen looked at Stevens and, at the sight of the sick expression, the sheriff kept his hand near his gun.

The well was uncovered. It had filled with debris to within a few feet of the top. The men were lowered with a coil of rope and started digging. Yoder stood on the brink of the well, fascinated, hypnotized. Frank, opposite him, glanced at the Pinkerton man with a feeling of triumph.

One of the men in the well suddenly yelled, 'Money! Gold!'

Stevens' face turned pale. He half turned but Jensen's gruff voice checked him. 'Just hold it right there.'

Stevens froze. He watched the activity around the well. The money sack had long since disintegrated and a man was sent racing to Owen Grange to get a new one. Shortly, the whole town, it seemed to Frank, formed an awed ring about the workers. The money was sacked, passed up and Owen Grange, dignity lost in excitement, counted it, Yoder hanging over him.

The banker looked up. 'A hundred dollars missing.'

'Fifty dollar gold pieces,' Frank said and looked down into the churned well bottom. 'Two coins could easily be lost in the dirt.'

'The banks will be happy,' Yoder said. He shook his head. 'How did you know?'

'Come to my office,' Frank answered with

a glance at the crowd. 'Bring Stevens. Ike, you may want to hold him.'

They crowded into the office. Stevens sank into a chair and stared dully at the money sack on Frank's desk. Jensen touched the rough canvas.

'Frank, how did you figure it?'

'Stevens told Nolan the money was hidden in town.'

'Sure,' Yoder cut in, 'but out of all places, how did you figure the well?'

'The timing. The actual robbers passed the money to Bailey. He passed it to Stevens, who hid it. At the trial it was brought out he was out of sight only a few minutes – not long enough to meet Bailey, ride out of town, hide the money and come back.'

Frank looked at Manuel. 'Ernesto was murdered that night. Right by the old well, but it was open then with nothing but a rotting curbing about it. Stevens was in the Cattleman the night of the robbery. Bailey came in and Stevens left. He was back shortly after.

'He knew no one came around the old well. He picked up the money where Bailey had temporarily hidden it – in an old barrel, maybe. He brought it to the well. A ladder or a rope would let him down. He covered the money with trash and came up. Ernesto's bad luck was that he came staggering along at that time and saw him.'

Manuel groaned as Frank continued. 'A drunken Mexican would tip the whole thing. Stevens knew it. A gun would make too much noise so he went after Ernesto with a knife. They fought and hit the rotten wood, broke it and nearly fell in. Stevens finally used the knife. He didn't have time to take care of the body. So he hurried back to the Cattleman. He had to wait for report of the robbery or the murder, or both. The murder came first.'

Frank looked at Stevens, who kept his head down, eyes on the floor. 'Stevens went to the well and Ernesto's body. He went through the motions of looking for sign. Then came word of the train robbery. Stevens did a nervy thing then. He ordered the broken curbing torn down and a cover put over the well. He knew he'd buried the gold deep under the debris, so there wasn't much of a chance it'd be found. He rode off with the posse.'

Frank shrugged. 'You know the rest. The cover was put on and everyone was glad that hole was covered. Actually, it was just one more way of hiding the money. It's stayed there for seven years in a place so familiar that no one ever thought of it.'

Jensen turned to Stevens. 'How about Ernesto?'

Stevens looked up. He had lost but he was resigned to it. He gave a wan, crooked smile and something of the old, sardonic laughter gleamed in his eyes. 'The Marshal has made a pretty good story. Point is, someone has to prove it.'

Manuel suddenly let out a howl of fury and lunged at Stevens. Frank, Dane and a couple of men grabbed him. He struggled a moment and then gave up. Jensen motioned Stevens toward the cells.

'We can try, I reckon murder's worth it. You'll stay here until I can take you to the county seat.'

Stevens slowly stood up. 'You're wasting the county's time and money.'

'Maybe. But if we don't hang you, the county'll be too hot for your safety. You can figure on that.'

Jed walked calmly to the cells.

Dane went home with Frank and they slept most of the day. That night, they went to the hotel. Peg had prepared a special supper and they ate hungrily. Peg wisely refrained from questions until the meal was finished, though she knew of the finding of the money and Jed's arrest. It had spread over the town like wildfire.

She saw Frank's proud glances at his brother and Peg knew the rift between them was gone for good. It added to the wonder of the question Frank had asked and she had answered in the kitchen when he had come out, ostensibly to help carry in the food.

The men finished at last and, replete, lingered over their coffee. She thought of Jed in the jail, waiting the trip to the county seat and the trial. 'Frank, will they find Jed guilty?'

'I doubt it. We know he did it – finding the money clinched that. But no one saw the fight or the knifing. There's so little evidence that the poorest lawyer could bring up the point of reasonable doubt.'

'Then he'll get off?'

'A chance – a good chance. But all of us have seen the last of him. If he ever came back to Apache Crossing, Manuel would kill him. It's all over, one way or another.'

'And you did it,' Dane said pridefully.

Peg reached across the table for Frank's hand. 'Why don't you tell Dane?'

Frank grinned and turned to his brother.

'How would you like Peg in the family?'

The boy laughed. 'I'd like it fine, now. I kept wondering all along when it would happen. Nothing like seeing a man happy with a beautiful woman. And when it's your own brother–'

Peg circled the table and, to Dane's surprise, put her arms about him and kissed him.

'Hey!'

Frank smiled when, startled, they looked at him. 'How come?'

'Jealous?' Dane laughed.

'Sure. After all, I'm the one she promised to marry!'

The publishers hope that this book has given you enjoyable reading. Large Print Books are especially designed to be as easy to see and hold as possible. If you wish a complete list of our books please ask at your local library or write directly to:

The Golden West Large Print Books
Magna House, Long Preston,
Skipton, North Yorkshire.
BD23 4ND

This Large Print Book, for people
who cannot read normal print,
is published under the auspices of

THE ULVERSCROFT FOUNDATION

... we hope you have enjoyed this book.
Please think for a moment about those
who have worse eyesight than you ...
and are unable to even read or enjoy
Large Print without great difficulty.

You can help them by sending a
donation, large or small, to:

**The Ulverscroft Foundation,
1, The Green, Bradgate Road,
Anstey, Leicestershire, LE7 7FU,
England.**
or request a copy of our brochure for
more details.

The Foundation will use all donations
to assist those people who are visually
impaired and need special attention
with medical research, diagnosis
and treatment.

Thank you very much for your help.